The Relevance of Men

ISBN: 1-4196-5150-1

To order additional copies, please contact us.
BookSurge, LLC
www.booksurge.com
1-866-308-6235
orders@booksurge.com

I. ALEXANDER
OLCHOWSKI

THE RELEVANCE OF MEN

2006

The Relevance of Men

This Book Is Dedicated To My Grandmother,
Who Gave Me Shelter To Write,
My Mother,
Who Imbued Me With Curiosity,
And Kino,
My Best Friend.

"The follies of everyday human life are much better entertainment than pretty much anything you can find on television. It's my job to combine the two."

\- Rupert Jones, NPR Reporter

THE RELEVANCE OF MEN

Eric Underwood drives his Toyota pickup along Reservoir Road. The aquatic biologist, with his scruffy black beard, slight belly and scratched glasses, wears well-worn things - a flannel shirt and blue jeans, leather belt with a rainbow trout buckle, brown suede work boots. His lower lip bulges with a fat pack of Skoal, the strongest chewing tobacco known to mankind. Besides cheap beer it's Eric's only real vice. Reaching the little dirt pull-off he parks the truck in the shade of an oak. He climbs out and lifts his scuba suit from the bed, then heads down a trail winding through the pine forest to the shores of Ashokan Reservoir, a vast lake holding over thirty percent of New York City's drinking water. Five minutes later he's stripped to his boxers and is stepping into a wet suit, sliding flippers onto his feet, adjusting the oxygen tank hookup. When everything is set he steps out into the water, carefully negotiating the slippery boulders. As the lake engulfs him, the frigid waters imperceptible through the artificial skin of the suit, his muscles relax. Once fully under water, Eric is completely at ease. It's a world he likes so much better than the terrestrial existence in which he's forced to spend most of his time living out. In his favorite novel, the last remaining humans after a nuclear holocaust devolve into dolphins, returning to a life in the ocean, the place from which all life originally emerged. Tomorrow, if given the chance, Eric would do the same, except he would choose some predaceous freshwater species; a northern pike or a giant water beetle. The ocean overwhelms him. Like outer space, the sea strikes him as a frontier people shouldn't feel the need to conquer. Eric Underwood is a freshwater man, a lover of lakes and streams, rivers and ponds.

He's recently left his job with the government funded DEC for a position with a leading consulting company in the race for the private acquisition of water supplies. His missions are often mundane, like today's, an investigation of the outlet pipes in the Ashokan Reservoir. Good at seeing the bright side of things, Eric is making double the salary of his old job with twice as much free time out in the field. It will take him less than ten minutes to check the pipes. But he'll end up spending the entire day at the reservoir, performing numerous dives that will have him underwater for over three hours. As usual, he'll let himself be swept away by the shy creatures and slanting beams of sunlight, the slippery plants waving back and forth in unseen currents, the heavenly floating silence of it all. And, as usual, he'll wish he could just stay under water forever, in the place he feels most himself.

When he gets back home to his bachelor's cabin that evening there is a message on his voice mail from the Japanese chemist he'd met at a recent conference. He has a flash of hope that she's calling to ask him out on a date. Then he listens to the recording.

Dr. Yomi Nguyen is finally alone. She knows all the other scientists have left the building. Her only company now is the security guard in the downstairs lobby and the night janitor roaming the floors with his squeaking cart of cleaning supplies. This is her favorite time of day. Yomi has nothing to go home to. She doesn't have a cat, or even a houseplant. The lab is home, work is her spouse, and Yomi prefers it that way. But although her job as a Developmental Chemist for Eli Lilly pays extremely well, it isn't the eight or ten daytime hours she puts in researching potential new antidepressants that brings her true satisfaction. After a quick dinner at her desk, usually instant Pad Thai in a paper cup, she watches the rest of her department head for the elevator. Only then does Yomi finally settle down into what she considers to be her true life's work.

Tonight, like every night, she strides down the stainless steel hallway, triggers open the glass suction door with her fingerprint, and steps into the sterile, steel laboratory. Once the door seals behind her she's alone. Void of human company, at least. The chimpanzees, shipped in from the jungles of The Congo, with DNA 97% identical to her own, provide her with more than enough companionship. They hoot and holler as Yomi heads straight over to their cage, a two-story mesh dome filled with tropical plants, humidifiers, and an artificial creek. Her experiments on the primates are always benign, ones Yomi would feel completely safe administering on human subjects. Her chimps are never treated poorly. She knows they are her allies, collaborators in her after-hours mission to discover a drug inhibiting the production of testosterone in human males; a highly potent, unique version of the drugs already developed, one she could administer to mass numbers in an efficient way. She's designed this particular inhibitor to target the hypothalamus, the region of the brain controlling production of the hormone in men. The necessary testosterone produced by the adrenal cortex, crucial to the nonsexual development of both men and women, will be unaffected by her drug. With men no longer producing the hormone that drives them toward power, women will finally assume control of humanity's ultimate destination. Working toward this goal is Yomi's purpose in life.

When she reaches the giant cage she remains encouraged by the visible evidence she's been waiting almost two decades to see. Since ingesting the latest version of her inhibitor a year earlier, the male chimps have been neglecting their normal roles of procuring food, disciplining the young, and maintaining overall order inside their contained paradise. They are content to simply lie beside the creek, napping off and on. And, unlike all of her previous test runs, the effect of the drug doesn't seem to be wearing off over time. She's given this one a substantial trial period, and still the male chimps are producing no testosterone. In reaction, just as Yomi's hypothesis predicted, the females have taken over control of the tightly knit, cage-bound society. She is certain that the shift to female dominance she's currently witnessing in these animals can be mirrored on a global scale, with men and women instead of chimpanzees. Acting on a rare impulse, Yomi heads immediately to the telephone and dials Eric Underwood's number. She plans to leave a message alerting him of her success and her desire to take him up on his offer to help. She holds her finger poised above the phone, hesitating before pressing the last digit of his number. Her nervous pause is something she's never experienced before. Reminding herself that she's not calling to ask him out on a date she completes the call. His answering machine picks up after a few rings.

Yomi hasn't allowed room in her life for anything resembling a crush since her freshman year of boarding school. Shortly after arriving at the polished Connecticut campus she made it her goal to win the affection of a worthy boy, hoping to get falling in love over with early, so she could concentrate on more important things. So while most of her freshman peers were reeling from the effects of living away from their parents at such an early age, she wandered through the upperclassmen dorms wearing miniskirts and tight tank tops. It didn't take her long to strike the fancy of Gary Nelson, a senior, and star quarterback of the football team. She let Gary woo her with picnics in the campus woods and late night stargazing sessions on the roof of the English building. Then came the first dance of the semester. They were the envy of the whole school, dancing together in perfect choreography, Yomi wearing a white flowing dress and Gary in a tuxedo. Afterwards they wound up alone in Gary's room, his roommate crashing elsewhere. In the fog of incense and Otis Redding, Yomi submitted to his experienced hands, happy to get the ordeal of first-time sex over with, convinced it would lead her directly into true love. Afterwards Gary rambled on and on about his upcoming football game that weekend, going so far as to sketch out the plays he hoped to accomplish in magic marker on the plywood supporting his roommate's mattress above them. Yomi couldn't call up the energy to respond when he finally asked her opinion. She felt no desire to stroke his ego during their afterglow. Something in her mind snapped as she realized that this would probably be what all men would want in the end. She would have no time for this. When he asked her if she loved him she couldn't pronounce the word no matter how hard she tried, a moment that marked the beginning of a curious speech impediment that would last for much of her life. The next day, after dumping Gary, she founded a club on campus called WHIP.

Only its female members knew what the acronym stood for – Women Have Inherent Power. They held weekly meetings in a dingy dormitory basement, feeding the fires of their idealistic feminism. They plotted the downfall of the cockiest jocks through a series of high profile embarrassing pranks, and organized a protest of the hidden disparities between the salaries of male and female professors by inciting a week-long student strike. In her junior year, however, Yomi had to turn over control of the club that had grown to be the most powerful social group on campus. The laboratory commitments of a straight-A chemistry student and future valedictorian left her with no time outside her studies for anything besides sleeping, eating, and jogging. Unlike most of her peers she didn't reserve any areas of her schedule for explorations of the opposite sex or experiences with various substances. After her semester abroad in Nepal, Yomi had the distinct sense that her life was going to be extraordinary. In this way, never veering from the discipline needed to maintain her direction, she has remained single and entirely unconcerned about men. And she hasn't had sex in almost two decades.

There in her lab, with the receiver pinched between her ear and shoulder, Yomi is glad when Eric's answering machine picks up after a few rings. His simple, direct words and husky voice make her momentarily speechless. She closes her eyes and focuses on the purpose of her call. When Yomi finally speaks, her tone has the calm certainty of a true scientist.

The next morning Eric is driving back to Ashokan. He suggested their initial dive should be in New York City's principal reservoir, where he'd been just the day before, because it seemed like the most logical place to start. At the conference where they'd met a couple months ago, what had been a gathering of scientists interested in water technology, Yomi had told him what she hoped to accomplish. She approached him over lunch on the last day of meetings, right after he'd given a lecture on the future of major city water supplies based on his current experiences working with the New York City sources in the Catskills. Less than a minute into their conversation Eric, once he got over her strange speech impediment of stumbling over certain "L" words, decided Yomi was the most focused and purpose-driven person he'd ever met. He could tell this from the look in her eyes, black eyes pinpointed on a goal, eyes that pierced him and everything else they focused on to the core. She told him how she wanted to change the world one man at a time.

"The men in positions of power over the last two thousand years have misused their natural driving force, testosterone, too many times, indulging in violence and greed and the selfish misuse of power – therefore, in my eyes, they've l-uff-ost the right to lead civilization – it's time for women to take over, and I'm going to make that possible – I just need your help to do it."

"Why me?" Eric asks. "Why are you even here, with all these hydrologist nerds?"

"Because . . . my drug is water soluble. And extremely concentrated. Get it?"

"I do."

Eric has no doubt Yomi will achieve her goal, whether he is the one who helps her or not. So after receiving her urgent message the night before it doesn't take him very long to decide. His only wish is that the fact that he's intensely attracted to her has nothing to do with his drastic decision, one that necessitates cutting all personal and professional ties for the indefinite future. He's aware that even the most honest, responsible man struggles to think with the mind instead of the body. But, as Eric likes to phrase it, he's good at putting his brain before his dick. He struggles daily to find positive outlets for his abundant sexual energy, activities that usually involve being under or near water, and considers himself an example that not all men mishandle this dangerously overwhelming hormone Yomi seems obsessed with. The only problem is that he finally feels ready to go for broke with a woman, to begin building a relationship that has the chance to last the rest of his lifetime. By this point in his life he's realized that all a woman really needs from a man is for him to be there, every day, like a rock or a tree. This is something Eric has never been able to do. Until a couple years ago he'd always been on the move, a wandering gypsy of a PHD, constantly uprooting himself in search of new ponds and puddles. Now he shows up every day for his career and goes home alone to the same one-man cabin every night, leaving his lakes and streams to the creatures that rightly inhabit them.

Yomi's car, a Honda hybrid, is already parked at the trailhead when he arrives in his pickup. Walking the same trail he followed the morning before, a trail he's negotiated so many times, Eric is surprised to find himself tripping over roots and stumbling on rocks. His legs are weak with nerves. It's not that he's intimidated by this extremely intelligent scientist - he knows he can hold his own in any arena of science. Eric is nervous because he hasn't been this attracted to a woman since the Spanish lepidopterist he wooed in graduate school, an affair as fleeting as a butterfly's life span. Now thirty-five years old, he's been trying to accept the fact that he might have to live out the rest of his life alone. He wonders if he's simply a dying breed. Fueled by maintaining a close relationship with the natural world, he was the last of his friends to get a cell phone or establish an e-mail account. He still doesn't have an Ipod. Whenever in a town or city he takes note of the people hurrying down sidewalks or riding in buses while seemingly talking to themselves. The first time he noticed these moving mouths his immediate thought was that maybe the nearby mental institute had just released its patients. Eric finds himself deeply disturbed by the reality that so much of American culture is defined by the nightly news. He's never had a television in his places of residence, yet feels driven to check into the news online just to stay in touch with his fellow countrymen. But now, having finally let go of his youth, he can't help worrying that maybe he's actually the dying breed of man, not the football-watching, violent movie-loving men he and Yomi are attempting to extinguish. So he's become adept at finding small pleasures in his days, taking peace from his silent bonding with aquatic creatures and feeling at home in their underwater worlds, the only place he truly fits in.

On the trail he slows his pace and contemplates turning around. How can he work alongside a woman he's so attracted to? The project might take years for them to complete, and he knows he won't be able to contain himself for that long. Yomi's sexiness, her elegant, petite body, long eyelashes and flashing smile, utterly belie her position as a laboratory nerd. When Eric finally emerges from the forest and onto the rocky shores of the vast lake he catches his breath. Yomi is even hotter in a bathing suit than his mind had let him imagine over the months since meeting her at the conference. She wears a pearl white bikini, and stands on a submerged boulder like a freshwater goddess from some myth he's never read. Her smooth brown skin glistens with beads of water. She grins into a beam of sunlight, lifting the snorkel and mask she's holding in one hand.

"You're l-uff-ate," she says, "so I made an initial survey while I was waiting for you to show up."

"Oh yeah?" Eric says, surprised by her spunkiness as he ducks behind some bushes. Stepping into his wet suit, his eyes pinned on what he can see of Yomi's exotic body through the brambles, he decides to roll with the situation, the way he used to treat life before he turned thirty, before there was anything to lose. By sunset the next day, if all goes according to schedule, millions of men in the greater New York City area will be essentially castrated forever. There is nothing to lose right now.

"All you have is that silly snorkel?" Eric fires back at her, stepping out of the bushes, zipping up his wet suit.

"Yup," she says. "Because I can hold my breath for three minutes, forty-two seconds!" she announces.

"Oh really?"

"Yes, really."

Once in the water any ice between them dissolves as Eric guides her through the world he knows so well. He points out different species of fish and aquatic vegetation while they go about the repetitive task of injecting her liquid drug into the outlet pipes submerged along one side of the lake. A few hours later, the inhibitor successfully deposited into twenty percent of New York's drinking water, the two scientists stand again on the rocky shoreline. Much of the underlying awkwardness from before has vanished, washed away by the fresh, clean water. Their eyes connect from behind the glass masks. When a bald eagle soars over their heads Eric can't help but take it as a sign. Right then and there, on the wild shores of New York City's largest reservoir, he pledges the next few years of his life to being her assistant. Then he asks her if she'll be making him drink her drug as well.

"Only if you want to . . .but you can be one of the lucky ones if you wish – we'll have to save some men to carry on the species. Just don't touch your tap water."

"I don't touch the stuff anyway."

"Good. It's bad for you. Come. We have to go – there are two more reservoirs to hit before the day is over."

Eric couldn't care less that it will be months before he even kisses his quirky partner. He lets Yomi set the pace of their romance, sleeping in a separate motel room without complaint as they work their way around New England and then down the East Coast. Moving towards the Mason-Dixon Line, castrating men by the millions, they giggle on the banks of secret paradises and skinny-dip under the stars in water no one is allowed to swim in. Eric brings maps of watersheds and municipal water sources. Having been granted a yearlong sabbatical from Eli Lilly, her chimps under the care of an unsuspecting colleague, Yomi carts along coolers full of her drug, enough of it to dose all of North America. They crash with friends, switch cars repeatedly, and camp out in the reservoir wildernesses for days at a time. And they make great efforts to ignore the newspaper and television reports of the mysterious illness debilitating the male population of the Northeast.

Eric's subtle attempts at initiating some kind of romance during these weeks are received but not returned by Yomi. While hiking into Quabbin Reservoir, Boston's main source of drinking water, inspired by the wild setting and the footprints of Henry Thoreau, Eric reaches out to take her hand on the trail. Thirty seconds later she wriggles her fingers free.

"I have a thing about sweaty hands," Yomi says, wiping her palm on her shirt. After finishing off Boston, a task that takes them over a week to accomplish, he picks a candlelit restaurant by the Common for a celebratory dinner. Once they're seated Yomi blows out the flame on their table.

"I'm not into candles, really," she says, without offering any further elaboration as she pulls out the aquifer maps for the Maine coast, eager to move into the next phase of their mission. A few days later, resting for a night in a lobster-fishing village, Eric borrows one of the skiffs docked in the tiny bay. After hauling the five-hundred-pound rowboat up an embankment and onto their car, he takes

Yomi out that evening for a surprise row into the bay beneath a full-moon eclipse. When she refuses to get out of the car to consummate Eric's dramatic date, he asks her why she doesn't want to go.

"It's just, I don't l-uff-ike watching the stars in a romantic way, that's all."

"Oh."

If her comment hadn't inspired a tidal wave of depression, Eric might have pointed out that his plan was to watch a full-moon eclipse, not the stars. This final blow to his wooing efforts knocks him down for a few weeks, during which time the two of them are extremely productive, until his attraction to Yomi overwhelms him once again.

Eric resumes his persistent courtship over the month it takes them to dose the Northeast, seizing any moment he can to crack the hard shell of his cohort. He picks her spontaneous bouquets of wildflowers, cooks her Pad Thai from scratch on his backpacker's stove, shares an ice cream cone with her on a town park bench. Yomi keeps her energy focused on their task at all times, allowing him to indulge in his seduction just enough to keep his spirits up, without letting his advances slow the pace of their progress. High on the rush of their success, they don't even notice how exhausted they are until they reach the Mid-Atlantic states, where their biggest challenge awaits them.

The group of priests prays and chants to their ancestors as the verdant green jungle creeps in from all sides, the plants listening in on the old prayer songs. The natives are gathered on the summit of *Gonawindua*, the sacred mountain epicenter of the Tayrona religion, one of the massive Sierra Nevada peaks located on the Caribbean coast of modern-day Colombia. These nature priests, men called *mamas,* are Indians indigenous to the region living in small villages scattered about the jungle-clad ridges and wild, sandy coves, a place they refer to as "The Heart of the Earth." From the accounts of the few western scientists who have been brave or crazy enough to study the area, there may be evidence proving them right. Fighting to protect their original lands from the daily threats of violence plaguing Colombia, the *mamas* believe that their intense prayer sessions, like this dawn ceremony at their most sacred site, are responsible for maintaining the health of the planet's entire ecosystem. After a millennia of carrying out this immense responsibility with relative ease, the elders are now finding that their job is growing exponentially more difficult with every passing year. Although they've yet to share it with the rest of their community, the six shamans gathered on the circular slab of stone are all deeply concerned about the situation. They can't help feeling that maybe the planet has already become too sick, that its heart is dying, and their singing merely a futile attempt at resuscitation. Speaking without talking, they make the unprecedented decision that by next year at this time they will have the help of a woman, a female priest from the modern world.

There are seven *mamas* in total, each representing one of the major villages scattered across the valleys notched between the mountains, two from each of the three native tribes inhabiting the Sierra Nevada. Only the Water Carrier, yet to reach the mountaintop, is not identified with a specific tribe. He is just below the summit, where he's courting the spirits of the highest freshwater spring in these mountains. This is an easy task for him. He's been doing it for more than fifty years, although this year will be his last. The next Water Carrier has already been chosen. His name is Juan Franco. Like all the shamans Juan spent the first nine years of his life in the dark, growing up blind in a pitch-black cave, subsisting on the food delivered once a day by his mother and the regular teachings of his elders. The world was built in his mind from descriptions whispered by the *mamas* who visited his cave every few days. After nine years in the dark he was finally allowed to emerge into the light of day. Reality was more beautiful than Juan's mind had ever been able to picture. Everything melted into layers of color, like living inside a Van Gogh painting. Being a *mama,* Juan sees reality as the world created by *aluna,* the original spirit of human thought. Forces that are out of the Indians' ability to influence with their ancient prayers now threaten this reality. The balance is shifting, tipping, soon to be lost.

Rupert Jones truly began his reporting career as a door-to-door vacuum cleaner salesman. He hadn't given up on journalism, even in the wake of internship after internship, none paying him more than fifty dollars a week. He simply came to the conscious conclusion that devoting a few years of his life to a trade like selling vacuums door-to-door, combined with his congenial Southern personality, would literally open the doors to thousands of contacts spanning every geographic, economic, and societal region in the country. He turned out to be the most successful salesman Electrolux had ever hired, winning Employee of the Year each of his three years with the company. They hated to see him leave, but knew the full-time job offer by NPR, following Rupert's independent report on the domestic tragedy of Katrina and the government's bungled response, was something he couldn't pass up.

Less than a month into the job, trying hard to make Washington D.C. feel like home, he receives a call from Marcia Sanderson, a repeat vacuum client from the Sacramento area. Rupert gets the call one evening in his downtown apartment while hanging posters of his heroes in an attempt to make the place feel like home, black and white shots of Malcom X, John Coltrane, Bob Marley. Rupert, far more comfortable in a bayou swamp than a big city, jolts at the sound of the ringing phone. He slides a couple windows down, hoping to block out the traffic noise, then answers the phone.

"Ullo?"

"Rupert! Marcia Sanderson – remember me?"

"Of course, Marcia. I remember all my clients."

"How are you, Rupi?"

"Oh wonderful, got my first real gig . . ."

"I know, I know, I heard you on the radio the other morning; you're a natural, Rupert – a better journalist than you were a vacuum salesman, and that's saying a lot."

"Why thank you, Marcia. So what's up?"

"What's up is that I might have the biggest tip you'll ever get in your entire career."

"Oh yeah? Let's hear it."

"You know who my neighbor is, right?"

"Of course – Jobs, the Ipod Baron – sorry to admit it, Marcia, but that's the reason you made my list of clients in the first place. I wanted to sniff him out a little."

"I figured as much, and I won't hold it against you. Anyway, you wouldn't believe what I'm watching from behind my living room curtains as we speak."

"What!?"

"Famous people, Rupi – the rich and famous are filing into his house one after another, and I'm talking heavy hitters – so far I've seen Oprah, Steven Speilberg, the Clintons, Bill Gates, Martha Stewart, Bob Dylan . . . "

"Okay, stop right there, something's goin' down, no doubt. I'm gonna' have to come camp out in your house for the weekend, Marcia . . ."

"If I hadn't known you were going to invite yourself, Rupert, I would have asked you to come much sooner in the conversation."

"Great, I'll be there in five hours."

"Rupi?"

"Yeah?"

"Can you bring me one of those fancy carpet attachments you tried to sell me?"

With access to NPR's highly sophisticated surveillance equipment, Rupert is able to listen in on most of the weekend's activities while hiding among the apricot trees surrounding Steve Jobs' Silicon Valley mansion. Saturday morning he spies on fifty of America's wealthiest, most renowned citizens gathered in the glass-walled conference room in the back of the house. To Rupert, what these fifty rich and famous people seem to have in common is a strong philanthropic spirit. The diverse group ranges from actors to musicians, politicians to home decorators, Tom Hanks to Elton John to Martha Stewart. Listening in on Jobs' speech to open the week-long meeting, Rupert hears how they've become members of the first sovereign nation lacking physical territory, with no place to build a capital or train an army. They believe in founding a new nation led by the freethinking, influential figures of American culture, a country that will head in an opposite direction from the world's new corporate-driven superpowers to guide the rebuilding of human society. He can't help wondering if they're nothing more than rich idealists with too much time on their hands. But either way, they seem quite serious.

This Saturday morning meeting, far from the beady eyes of the press, is to assess their resources and outline a specific game plan for moving forward. Jones gathers from the meeting's undercurrents that the catalyst behind this serious meeting is the U.S. government's overall indifference to the Carolina disaster, yet another tropical storm of serious magnitude to lash into the Southern Coast, continuing a string that began with Katrina. The response from Washington to each and every storm has brought to light the current reality that the rich and powerful take care of their own and disregard the poor and downtrodden in a time of abject need. This is what has driven these philanthropists to finally make this leap, something they've all been contemplating for years. Rupert can see right away that the chances for success are high. They're starting out with more available cash reserves than any other nation in the world, not a single debt and, as of yet, no population to take care of. And they are fifty of the most effective, successful people on the planet.

Once Jobs finishes his opening speech he calls the blonde Senator of New York and former first lady, unanimously elected as president of this infant nation, to step up in front of the giant monitor. After a steady round of applause she receives with class and grace, Hillary Clinton beams her laser pointer at number one and smiles. *Have Fun* reads the yellow print on black background.

"This goal, given the makeup of our initial body of citizens, shouldn't be very hard to achieve – am I right?"

Billy Crystal makes a dramatic farting sound with his throat and the room bursts out in raucous laughter. Hillary moves the laser down to number two – *Land.* Lacking any physical territory in which to base their new country is a factor that had initially been considered an advantage. Now being a homeless nation is quickly turning out to be a distinct weakness. Hillary announces the group's decision to use a quarter of their two-hundred-billion dollar operating budget on the acquisition of a substantial piece of land within a cooperating country, a requirement that immediately rules out the United States of America. Hillary addresses the group in her calm, professional voice. Rupert, gorging himself on perfectly ripe apricots out in the orchard, presses on the ear piece in an effort to catch all her words.

"Later this afternoon we will be hearing proposals on three different potential geographic locations, scouted by various members of our Land Search Committee over the past month and a half. Then we'll take a vote!"

The proposed locations are listed in yellow on the outline: *British Colombia (Canada), Argentina, and Fiji.* Hillary moves the pointer down to the third objective of the weekend meeting - *An Armed Force.* It's a common aspect of nations that the group had been hoping to avoid, planning to emulate Costa Rica and Panama, to be known as a peace-loving country interested in maintaining a foreign policy that doesn't involve the use of force.

"As all of us know," Mrs. Clinton continues, "corporations are beginning to share the militaries of the nations they pay their taxes to – this is a deeply disturbing situation – but it doesn't mean we have to play their game. It's risky, but we have to give it a shot – so in case some form of military response is needed at some point, Mr. Cristopher Walken will be in charge of developing this area."

A general hush follows a quick round of applause as the risky concept of building a nation without an army truly sinks in. The actor whose face shines with an icy cool shoots a confident wink out at the entire room. The fourth and final objective is *Dr. Yomi Nguyen.* Below the Japanese scientist's name is the following – *Water Soluble Testosterone Inhibitor.* It's obvious from the amount of whispers being passed back and forth that the founding members have heard nothing about this last topic.

"Our Intelligence Operative, the person you all voted never to meet, convinced me to add this last objective to the list – it seems that Dr. Nguyen has just discovered a method for delivering a testosterone inhibitor drug, with permanent effects after only the slightest contact with the system, into city water sources. The motives behind her decades long, secretive pursuit of this goal remain a mystery, and her plans for using it unknown."

Hillary takes in a deep breath as she clicks off the monitor and steps up to the edge of the great table. Rupert almost drops the long-range microphone.

"I'm sure that everyone here can imagine the potential implications of the ensuing scenario – "

"We sure as hell can!" shouts Oprah, pounding a fist on the table as she rises from her seat. "Our day has come, ladies! I say it's about time for the boys to hand over the reins!"

She stares down every man in the room one at a time.

"Am I right?"

A steady round of applause rises, a sustained clapping by both sexes, forcing Rupert to yank out his ear piece. Clutching his aching stomach full of peaches he scuffles back to Marcia's house under the cover of a soft California dusk.

Rupert Jones has to leave Silicon Valley early the next morning to pursue coverage of another meeting taking place this same weekend. NPR doesn't know he's attending this one either, a gathering that's being broadcast across every major television channel in the country. The public network thinks he's on his way to cover the aftermath of the Carolina hurricane and its shady connection to the exponential skyrocketing of fuel prices. But Rupert, on the bottom of the totem pole of NPR reporters, stuck on the radio even as the network branches into television, is eager to break out. A cautious foray initially undertaken simply to offer the nightly news watchers an informed alternative to the biased trend initiated by the Fox Network, NPR has quickly become the most watched news channel on T.V. Using their newfound budget wisely, the network's penetrating investigative journalism suddenly finds itself with an audience a hundred times larger than its radio broadcasts had ever reached. As the new NPR president understands well, even the most politically open-minded Americans find comfort from television, especially in the evenings after a long day at work. Along with the rest of the network's board he struggles with the decision to go corporate, how to handle all the cash flow, and the pressure of being looked up to by millions of intelligent people with good intentions.

At least for now, Rupert wants to protect the secret of New America, largely because he believes in it. So he puts that story on the back burner, and focuses on the array of connections from his vacuum sales days who are tipping him off to other newsworthy secrets left and right. Some contacts in the bayou have told him about a weather-making machine the conservative majority have funded the development of, a system they've designed to create the string of tropical storms that have battered the southern coast over the past few years, giving their companies an excuse to drive up gasoline prices. Rupert is planning on investigating this lead when he finally does make it south next week. And then there is the former client employed by Eli Lilly who just filled him in on the secret experiments of the Japanese chemist mentioned at Job's mansion. He's come to this meeting hoping to let that particular cat peak it's head out of the bag.

The conference is a meeting of the newly formed, congressionally appointed Alliance of Corporate Partners. Wandering through the presentation room with pine board walls, cowering beneath the stuffed heads of large game animals hanging in frozen expressions of terror, Rupert can't believe he's been granted entrance to the Midwest ranch, getaway of the current U.S. president. The back of the room is filled with leather couches, glass tables, and swivel chairs. Cigar smoke mingles with bourbon fumes; Republican majority leaders with the CEO's of some of America's largest corporations. The Alliance is the current President's idea, bringing a union that has existed quietly for decades out into the open in hopes of giving America a powerful one-two punch in its race against China and India to secure the world's rapidly vanishing natural resources. The president takes the podium in front of an enormous bank of windows revealing fields of wheat and corn stretching out to the horizon. He drinks from his glass of water, then coughs softly into the microphone. The hobnobbing in the back ceases. The members of the press, seated in metal chairs up front, snap to attention. Cameras flash. News feeds role.

"Good evening, America, and God bless our great nation. As you are all aware, we are living in a changing world. This means we are being forced to blur the lines between government and business, and are gathered in this room today to unite our collective resources, to brainstorm on a game plan to secure energy and food that will last for our citizens well into future generations."

The CEO's and officials put down their drinks to clap and hoot and holler in response. The president nods down at the press section, employing one of his practiced smiles.

"Now I'll answer a few questions."

Hands shoot up in the air. He picks a reporter he recognizes from the network most sympathetic to his agendas.

"Mr. President, sir, what qualifications, if any, does a corporation need to have in order to become a member of the Alliance?"

"The requirements for membership are simply an annual operating budget over one hundred million dollars, the expressed desire to fully support American foreign policy goals around the world, and a strong faith in the Lord God Our Father."

More hands are raised. The president picks another from the sympathetic network's online affiliate.

"Sir, if the businesses are expected to give blanket support to U.S. policy objectives, what, to put it bluntly, is in it for them?"

The president shifts his weight, dodging the blow thrown only to make him look like he's on his toes.

"Good question, Mike, and I'm very glad you brought it up – the fine corporations represented here today will all be receiving certain . . .benefits at home – which will be detailed in the charter we plan to draw up this weekend, and available for public viewing immediately."

Rupert rises in the back row of chairs. Knowing the president would never call on him, he doesn't bother to raise his hand, but instead shouts out a question that interrupts the nation's leader in the midst of calling on another approved reporter seated up front.

"Mr. President, sorry to interrupt, sir – "

"I would expect nothing less of a representative from your network, Mr. Jones."

Another false grin follows, this one to raucous applause from the corporate hogs in the back half of the great room. Rupert hesitates for a nervous second, then regains his composure. The president raises his palm apologetically.

"Now that you have everyone's attention, though, you might as well proceed."

Rupert, sweating more profusely than he ever did peddling vacuums across the Moab Desert in an old Ford Escort, clears his throat before speaking.

"Mr. President, sir, I would like to ask you what the Alliance's stance might be on the recent discovery, by an American scientist incidentally, of a method of administering a drug permanently blocking the production of testosterone in male chimpanzees to mass numbers of men?"

Rupert intentionally leaves out the specifics of this method. Although his loyalties are placed solely in truthful reporting, if he had to choose a side his allegiance would be to Yomi without question, even though he has yet to meet her. It's about time someone is shaking up an old system that's no longer working. So he hopes his vagueness will keep the government hogs off their trail for the time being. In the wake of silence created by his question every pair of eyes in the room is focusing on Rupert. All eyes except the President's. His glance darts about haphazardly. He chuckles awkwardly into the microphone. His forehead scrunches up and his mouth tightens into a forced smile. Then he asks two questions that, coming from the mouths of most leaders, would have been taken as a joke. Coming from this president's lips, however, they all know he's perfectly serious.

"What is testosterone, Mr. Jones, and why should I care?"

Rupert Jones, still getting over his surprise that the president knows him by name, doesn't have to say another word. His purpose has been achieved. He sits back down. The other reporters drop their hands and murmur among themselves. The president is visibly agitated by the situation. TV cameras are shut off or pointed at the floor. The back of the room is utterly silent.

"What?" the president asks in an extra thick accent, defending his blind ignorance with another false smile and a casual shrug of his shoulders. His advisors have told him over and over that when all else fails he should try to look as cute and endearing as possible. Desperately craving a hug from his wife, he steps down from the podium and walks out a side door. Following his exit the reporters come to a quick agreement that the testosterone story won't be leaked any time soon, if ever. They huddle around the NPR reporter, eager to know more details of what he's talking about. But, loyal to this brave and mysterious scientist, Rupert keeps this information to himself. With a sly grin on his face he walks out the door, satisfied that he's stirred things up just enough, eager to see what the nightly news will have to say about it all.

Mark Reynolds returns home to his suburban mansion in Greenwich on Friday evening. It's been a long day at the office and he needs a drink. Pulling into the driveway he notices that his wife's car is gone. She must be picking up their boys at some extracurricular activity, he thinks, walking up the path through the manicured grass of his front yard, carrying his briefcase and that day's issue of the Wall Street Journal. As he unlocks the front door Reynolds is hoping his wife has made fresh ice cubes today. He likes his Johnny Blue with three rocks, and he likes the ice to be recently frozen. Over the course of his law career, forced to attend thousands of cocktail parties, he's learned how to notice the differences in the melting of a week-old cube versus one made a few hours before. The transition from solid to liquid goes so smoothly when the cube is fresh. Like his job, good scotch is all about smooth. Mark Reynolds is known as the smoothest lawyer in Manhattan. He's so fluid opposing lawyers shudder when they see him enter the courtroom. Being undefeated for his career and having won over five hundred cases has earned Mark the respect from judges all the way up to the superior court. He has to turn down cocktail and dinner parties weekly, usually because he needs to spend the extra time at his office. Driven by success and leaving no room for failure, Mark feeds off his identity as the sole provider for his growing family. Although he rarely even sees his wife and children, their reliance on him is present all day, pushing him up and up through the ranks of his field as he rises higher and higher, on pace with the skyscrapers of The Big Apple.

Reaching into the freezer Mark is delighted to see that the ice is freshly frozen. He can tell by the clarity of the cubes. He drops three of them into a rocks glass and makes his way into the den. At his bar in the corner he pours a double shot of the high-end booze over the ice and settles into his leather chair with the *Journal* and his drink. Crossing his legs, flipping open the front page and taking his first delicious sip, Mark feels like a man. He made fifteen hundred dollars today, and here he is in his sacred leather chair before five o'clock. The soothing aromas of a baking chicken begin to spill in from the kitchen. Mark is utterly content. An hour later he's finished the paper and the drink. Uncrossing his legs to steady himself he begins to feel extremely mellow, an opposite effect from what his Friday evening scotch usually produces. He normally can't wait to talk to his wife, feeling like he has a hundred things to tell her about his day. And, usually, he's already looking forward to sleep, eager for the morning, his most productive time, to come sooner. Right now he feels similar to the way he did after smoking marijuana those few times in college. He sits still, enjoying the sensations passing through him. His thoughts shed their usual anchors, his identities as a husband, a father, and a lawyer. His mind lifts up into abstraction. He closes his eyes and surrenders to the warm waves of color and feeling bathing his extremities in rhythm with his bloodstream. He wants to be outside, in the backyard he's never really set foot in, lying on his back watching the stars. Mark Reynolds never thinks about the stars.

Driving home to their house in Greenwich, with her two boys in the back seat, Sara Reynolds isn't exactly looking forward to arriving. Her favorite day of the week, by far, is Sunday. By then her husband finally relaxes enough for his company to be enjoyable, for her to feel the spark of love he inspired when they'd met a decade before, when his passion for law school, diligent work ethic, and ritual habits had swept her away into the marriage she'd been waiting patiently for since adolescence. Now a decade into his career, Mark has developed a steadfast predictability that often times, although she would never show it, drives Sara crazy. Tonight he'll drink his scotch on the rocks while he reads the *Journal*, expounding about his day as if what he did with it was the most important event in the world, then nodding absently while she tells him the details of her own day. After eating her homemade dinner, their half-an-hour to feel like a real family, he'll retire to the living room to watch old movies on cable. Tomorrow, Saturday, after rising at dawn to work all morning at his desk it will be off to the gym, where Mark will finally start to expel his week's worth of energy. Then there will usually be a cocktail or dinner party to attend in the evening. Finally, on Sunday, he will be all hers. On Sunday she will get to keep him in bed late for their programmed, once-a-week lovemaking session. Then she'll choreograph the rest of his day, booking his attention for blocks of time as if she were one of his clients. Sara can often convince herself that she's happy on Sundays, a feeling that dissolves by Monday night, while she struggles to stay awake for his late-night return from the office.

The front door opens. Mark can hear the voices of his wife and boys. He snaps his eyes open and focuses on the rocks glass sitting on the coffee table, a tiny sip of watered down scotch remaining in the bottom. He smacks his lips together and slides his tongue across his teeth, trying to investigate the source of his strange mood. Ever since his days as a line cook during summers off from college, when the head chef had him taste every sauce and reduction created in the kitchen, Mark has been aware of his acute sense of taste. But the scotch has the same smoky caramel flavor that it always does. He hears his children bound up the stairs to their TV's and video games. His wife stands in the doorway to the den.

"Honey, did you do something funny to the ice when you made it?" Mark asks. He's thinking about standing up to greet her but is unable to initiate any kind of movement.

"No, dear, I just filled up the trays from the tap like I do every Friday afternoon before you get home - I know how much you like the fresh ice cubes in your drink."

She approaches his chair and bends down to kiss him on the lips. Mark pulls away.

"What's wrong?"

"I don't know, I feel . . .funny"

"Too funny to kiss me?"

"Yes."

His wife strokes his gray hair.

"Maybe you just need a nap, dear – close your eyes and relax – there."

He obeys her directions without argument. She continues running her fingers through his hair as he drifts off into sleep. Then she rises, picks up his glass and smells it. Shaking her head, she goes into the kitchen, where she pulls the ice trays from the freezer and empties them into the sink. She decides tomorrow morning she'll call a spring water company to begin making regular deliveries, like some of her friends have been thinking of doing ever since one of them read an article on the health risks of municipal tap water a few months ago. Sara has no way of knowing it, of course, but just like her friends she is already too late to save her husband from the drug, one Dr. Yomi Nguyen designed to be permanently effective after even the slightest contact with the internal system.

After drinking the scotch with the mysterious aftertaste Mark Reynolds sleeps for over fourteen hours. His wife finally rouses him at ten o'clock. By then he's usually three or four hours into his Saturday morning desk work and ready to head for the gym or tennis club. Today he groans as Sara shakes him awake. Once fully conscious, he notices her look of intense concern.

"What's wrong, sweetheart?" he asks, wearing a goofy grin.

"What's wrong with you, dear? It's after ten o'clock in the morning!?"

Mark sits up on the pillows and shrugs his shoulders.

"Don't you have work to do?" she asks him.

"Work? What's that?"

Sara slaps him on the leg.

"Don't tease me, Mark! I'm really worried about you – you've worked every Saturday morning for the past decade!"

"Well, not today - today I'm making you breakfast in bed!"

"Oh really?"

His sudden spontaneity is taking Sara slightly off guard. She tries to roll with it.

"And what are you going to make me to eat?"

"I'll figure that out when I get into the kitchen," Mark states.

"Well, aren't you fun today . . ."

His expression drops instantly.

"I'm not usually fun?"

She moves to kiss him. He turns away, not interested in her advances.

"No, sweetheart, I'm not saying that. It's Saturday, that's all – you're always working Saturday morning, as far back as I can remember, anyway . . ."

Mark slips away from her and climbs out of bed. He dresses haphazardly.

"Well, there's nothing wrong with a little change, is there?"

Sara shakes her head.

"The kitchen is calling," he says, leaving his wife in bed, rejected and utterly confused by the man she thought she knew so well until this morning.

In the kitchen a phone call interrupts Mark in the midst of mixing buttermilk pancake batter.

"Mr. Reynolds, please," requests a female voice.

"Speaking. And you are?"

"Secretary to the president, sir."

"President of . ? ."

"The United States, sir."

"Oh, well, I'm pretty busy right now . . .what can I do for you?"

Mark pinches the phone to his shoulder in order to pour his first pancake into the skillet.

"The president would very much like to meet with you at your earliest convenience, to discuss a potential lawsuit. You were referred to us as the first choice."

"Well, thank you . . . but I'm going to have to decline your offer. Have a fine day, though."

He hangs up the phone to continue coordinating his breakfast efforts.

"What was that all about?" Sara shouts down from the bedroom.

"Nothing important," Mark shouts back. "Are you getting hungry?"

In the kitchen Mark takes note of his newfound sensibilities for food. His fingers handle the eggs with soft tenderness, cupping them gently while cracking the shell with a fork. He mixes the pancake batter with his hands, enthralled by the texture, his skin tingling with warm, sensuous feeling as the batter bubbles from heat in the teflon pan, dancing in splatters over the edge. Blueberries sit in a ceramic bowl close to the action, ready to be called upon. A beam of morning light strikes the recently washed berries, glancing off the round, wet edges. Mark gets lost in the dance of it all, in the one-man twirling culinary ballet.

By the time he's finished the blueberry pancakes, bacon, eggs and toast breakfast, batter on the floor and grease on the walls, Mark has reached a state of domestic bliss unattainable for a normal, testosterone producing man. High on this plateau of house-husband contentment, he hardly feels the stairs under his feet as he bounds up them to feed his wife her breakfast in bed, a bed the two will never make love in again.

On the same Friday evening Ben Clarkson is walking back to the cabin he shares with his wife in the mountains of southern Vermont. He's spent the day out in their woods selectively harvesting trees for a little supplementary income while managing the growth of a healthy forest at the same time. He makes a stop at the well to fill up one of the five gallon jugs stacked beside the old pulley-and-bucket system. He lays his chain saw, sticky with sap, down on the soft ground beside his feet. The spring he built before he even started on the house is a classic one, complete with a tiny, V-shaped roof to keep out debris and a tall, circular wall of stone and mortar to keep out curious kids and thirsty animals. After filling the jug with buckets of fresh spring water he climbs the trail criss-crossing up the backside of the hill, up towards their log home perched on a forested plateau. His wife Maria, rector of the Evangelical Church in Brattleboro, will soon be arriving from another trail, one that links the house to their driveway at the base of the small mountain. Once inside Ben drops the chain saw in the mudroom, carries the water jug into the kitchen, then moves into the living room to feed the wood stove.

During his days in the woods, with only his border collie Al for company, Ben rarely thinks about his wife. But once inside the snug embrace of their home, his day's work done and the evening's work just beginning, his thoughts wander often to Maria. With a fire up and roaring in the cast-iron stove, he lowers their hidden stairs and climbs down into the root cellar to collect potatoes and onions for that night's dinner. Ben splits the wood and makes the fires, hauls the water, plants the seeds, harvests the fruits of the garden, and prepares most of their meals. He brings his wife down from the precipitous heights of the spiritual world she spends so much of her time dwelling in, connecting her to the earth by the way he sustains their home. He often thinks she might fly away like a kite if he let her go for even a second. While Ben holds things together on this practical, earthy level, Maria's intense spiritual connection keeps them both linked to the gods and saints. Her potent prayers ensure that when their lifestyle of self-sufficiency seems too hard to bear, the load will be lifted from their shoulders just in time. In this way she lifts him with her, giving their dreams wings and carrying them to good places all night long, until songbird angels sing the next day awake.

While Maria drives the mud-rutted road that winds up from Brattleboro, heading home to their spot in the hills above Newfane, the day fades slowly into night. She keeps glancing down at the passenger seat, where an international envelope rests. The letter inside, penned on wide-ruled paper in simple English, arrived in her office mailbox that day. The return address of Santa Marta, Colombia, S.A., intrigued her even before she'd read the unexpected note while standing in her wooden pulpit before all the empty pews. Written collectively by a group of shamans living in the mountains of Northern Colombia, the letter is a passionate plea that has been sent to a thousand female religious leaders in North America, all of various faiths and chosen at random. The shamans are asking for help in their primary task of praying for the health of the planet. Maria absorbs the letter's content deeply, and it stays with her through the rest of the day. She can't wait to read it again, out loud to her husband that evening.

After parking in the driveway she climbs the trail to their house slowly, taking time on the way to shed the day's work, stopping here and there to breathe in the ground as it wakes to a chorus of spring peepers. In Vermont, winter's grip is strong and long lasting, making its death all that much sweeter, a funeral accented by fleeting flowers, flavored with maple syrup. Maria smiles as she finally steps up to the solid oak door lit by a hanging oil lantern. Stepping into the cozy comfort of their home she shakes off the slight chill that had slipped into her during the walk. She's embraced by the dirt-scented steam of boiling root vegetables, the wood stove warmth, and her husband. She pulls the letter from the pocket of her fleece jacket. Ben steps back.

"What's that?"

"Have a seat," Maria says, soft but firm. "I'll read it to you."

Ben knows when she's serious. He sits at the maple table he built with his own hands the year before. She stands before him, opens the letter, and starts reading in her sermon voice.

Mrs. Clarkson,
We are contacting you, and other women of faith from your country, to ask for help. The Earth is changing in bad ways. We, the Tayrona people, are responsible for maintaining the balance of Mother Earth with our prayers. We have done this for centuries, but can no longer do it alone. Although the religions of your country are much different than ours, prayer is prayer, and there is great power in cooperation. We are asking you to come here and help us pray, to stay as long as you can, to help us give the planet a chance to survive. The first one to respond will be welcomed as our honored guest.

Sincerely,
The Tayrona Mamas
(Guardians of the Heart of the Earth)

By the time she finishes reading the letter Maria's eyes have a wild look.

"I want to go – and I want you to come with me!"

Ben's shoulders sink. The thought of leaving behind his books, his woods and his dog for any length of time weighs heavy on him.

"I don't want to leave," he says, staring down at his table, mad at himself for sounding like a child. "I'm sure someone's already responded by now anyway – "

"I did – I emailed their contact in Santa Marta right after I read the letter, and I was the first one to write back, so they invited me and I accepted – you can decide on your own if you're coming, but I'll need to know soon."

The bluntness of her statement shocks him. Stunned and numb, Ben moves into the kitchen to check on his stew, hoping the aromas of boiling meat and potatoes will restore feeling to his extremities.

Ben has a place he goes to first thing almost every morning, a view he cut out of the woods on one flank of their mountain, a small plateau occupied primarily by a rock perfect for sitting on. The next morning Ben sits here longer than usual. He doesn't come here to pray, exactly, simply to take it all in, to feel reverence. The land contained in the view is sprawling acres of state forest and family tracts to be passed down one generation at a time, Vermont-style. After years of observation he knows the only thing that changes about the view are the colors. The farmhouses, their adjacent fields and expanses of forest, stay mostly the same. It's the colors that change, in a slow- motion shift from the deep spinach greens of mid-summer, to reddish orange becoming crinkled brown and fading yellow, to a coat of white blanketing it all for the long nap of winter. After all the blacks and browns of mud season comes lime green spring to start the circle all over again. Ben watches this color wheel turn, reveling in the near permanence of the view from his rock, pretending life can be put on hold, fooling himself into thinking change can be confined to a landscape. In the back of his head Ben knows how good he is at hiding from change, hanging on to the comfortable. His mother was in labor for thirty-eight hours because his developing body clung to the safe haven of her womb. To go to Colombia, to be away from his books and his root cellar for an extended period of time, is a painfully daunting prospect. He will have to force himself to go, just like he makes himself get up off the rock every morning, leaving his view to get on with the day. At least he'll be with is wife. She'll make it all okay.

Following the initial meeting at Jobs' mansion the group of fifty original New America citizens takes the next three weekends to investigate the potential locations narrowed down by their search committee. Making their own plans to get there, they meet first in Argentina, where they feast on cheap steak and red wine after touring the large tracts of pristine, dirt cheap land. The steak eaters and Spanish speakers among the group, a definite minority, feel right at home, while the rest of the group is put off by the slight undercurrent of cockiness in the Argentinean people. The next weekend they all meet in Fiji, where they check out an uninhabited archipelago surrounded by beds of virgin coral. The snorkelers and sun-worshippers think they've found home. But most of the group is hooked on the Northern Hemisphere, on the familiar angles of light and the fluctuating seasons. So when they meet up the third weekend on the great plains of southern British Columbia, the landscape strikes almost every one of them as the best place to pull off what they're trying to do. At a Sunday afternoon barbecue, catered by Vancouver Culinary Adventures under a great tent on the rolling fields, a vote is taken on the three locations. British Columbia, although the most expensive piece of property by far, easily earns the majority vote required. A deal is brokered in Vancouver the following morning, and construction on the first fifty underground living spaces begins that week.

New America is like no other country in the world. All dwellings are built into the earth with skylight windows, leaving the surface ground free for things like greenhouses full of hydroponic gardens, a giant community dining hall, and performance arenas for theatre, film, and music. With the gates open to all immigrants who pass a specific application process, the virgin nation's population quickly swells to over a hundred thousand. Almost everyone lives underground. Thousands of acres of open territory are permanently protected as wilderness. The governing body, something agreed to at the tail end of the meeting at Steve Jobs', is a group of women known as The Inner Circle. They will soon hold a series of sessions in their underground meeting chambers to come up with the country's constitution. But first the chambers, to resemble a womb, have to be constructed.

At the nation's temporary headquarters, what is so far simply a series of tents on platforms made of recycled bottles, Hillary Clinton pauses her pacing to listen to Madonna's angelic voice ringing out across the plains. The singer has been giving impromptu concerts with Elton John beside the grand piano he's set up in a bowl of rolling, grass-covered hills. Just as the melodic piano melody swells up a ringing cell phone interrupts Hillary's appreciation of the music. She clicks on her head set.

"Yes?"

"This is intelligence, Mrs. President."

The voice is low and smoky. Even Hillary has never met their mysterious spy, the former Navy Seal.

"Go ahead," she says.

"The pair of scientists is injecting their testosterone drug into the water supply of every major city along the East Coast. And we think they're headed towards D.C."

"What are the effects?" Hillary asks.

"On males the effect is basically castration. The effects on females will be negligible. But right now they seem to be stalling – the White House appears to be a very daunting prospect for them."

Hillary paces about among the tents. She speaks her thoughts out loud into the phone.

"I can help them, maybe – I know a thing or two about the White House, and I still have friends there . . ."

Hillary pauses, realizing she's not sure if she wants them to be successful. But that's her own problem. Her spy has done his job.

"Listen, good work. Keep it up, okay?"

"I plan on it, Mrs. President."

Yomi and Eric's honeymoon phase is over. Sitting in the Bethesda, Maryland bus terminal, grimy from three days in the hills scouting out Baltimore's drinking water sources, Yomi sleeps on Eric's substantial shoulder while he flips through the latest issue of *Thirst*, his favorite magazine, one devoted entirely to global water issues. Most of the crusty, bloodshot eyes in the terminal are fixed on the mysterious couple with damp hair and scratched skin and mud-soaked clothes. Yomi squirms awake. She's sore and exhausted.

"How are we ever going to get into the White House well?" she says with soft, sleepy urgency. Even with millions of men already castrated around the Northeast, for Yomi their initial success hinges on whether they'll be able to dose the president, a man who exemplifies the reason she began the project decades before. Eric shakes his head slowly.

"I have no idea."

"I feel like we're being watched – listened to – "

"Don't be paranoid."

Yomi scans the room, searching for mysterious, secret service types, going by images from movies of men in dark suits and darker glasses. There are no such men in the Besthesda bus terminal.

"How are we going to do it?" she asks him again, knowing he doesn't have the answer. Eric has actually been arguing that maybe dosing the president, and his cabinet and advisors, isn't as important as she thinks it is. Yomi won't even discuss this possibility. She feels adamant that the current leader of their country is the exact kind of man she's driven to neutralize once and for all. Eric can make no counter-argument. He feels the same way about their shortsighted president and the people he's surrounded himself with. A man sitting beside them angles his newspaper to one side. They see that Robert Redford has been there the entire time listening in on their conversation, his face hidden from their repeated surveys of the room behind the newspaper and wide-brimmed cowboy hat.

"Someone wants to help you," he whispers.

"Really?" Yomi says, the wistful tone of a slight cinematic crush in her voice. The movie star nods, stroking the scruff of his face, his skin worn red by the Utah air.

"Don't take your bus south – once its left the terminal, I will get up and walk out that back door over there - you guys will go out the front, and I'll pick you up there."

"What do you drive, Mr. Redford?" Yomi asks in a whisper.

"Please call me Robert."

"Okay."

"I drive a Hummer."

Yomi lifts her eyebrows.

"Hydrogen powered, of course," Redford adds along with a smooth tip of his cap.

"So where will you be taking us?" Eric stammers, unable to hide the twinge of jealousy behind his voice.

"To meet with the leader of the newest country on the planet. Her name is Hillary Clinton."

Rolling east in a brand new car, heading towards D.C., the scientist couple is optimistic about their prospects following their secret meeting with Hillary Clinton in the Maryland countryside. With blueprints to the White House plumbing system, obtained by Hillary from friends still holding positions there, maids and chefs the president never thought to change upon taking office, they seem poised for success in what will be their biggest challenge yet. And with the secret sponsorship of New America, what had been the final outcome of the meeting, the rest of their mission is almost guaranteed to go smooth and unhindered now that they have access to a virtually unlimited budget. At the White House gates their roles are clearly defined. Eric is dressed up as a homeless wacko, a white sign hanging from his neck on which he's scribbled nonsensical words in black magic marker. His goal is to employ his acting skills, leftover from college drama classes, in an attempt to attract the attention of the secret service manning their posts outside. Distracted by his antics, the hope is that they'll leave the back gardens unwatched, allowing Yomi, wearing a camouflage wetsuit and carrying a loaded syringe, an opportunity to reach the well.

Their execution is almost flawless. Yomi rappels a hundred feet down into the well and successfully injects her drug. But while emerging from under the manhole cover she's confronted by a man with a beer belly piloting a ride-on lawnmower. The grounds crew member they hadn't accounted for in their planning cuts off the machine and approaches Yomi before she has a chance to slip over the back fence. As she pulls off her mask he moves closer, his intrigue and curiosity drawing him in. Yomi glances down at the syringe and sees that she didn't use all of the potent liquid. She smiles coyly at the maintenance man.

"Can I help you, ma'am?" he asks, stepping up to face her.

Yomi nods, flicking her eyelashes and smiling as seductively as she can. When the man takes a step closer she plunges the syringe into his beer belly, injecting the rest of its contents, then dashes off towards the back fence as he doubles over, screaming. The high concentration of her drug sends the only witness to her crime into convulsions that culminate in a gruesome death accented by feminine screams and shriveling testicles.

As Yomi climbs over the back fence Eric is being led out the front gate by a horde of secret service men in agreement that he's too insane to bother arresting.

"The Apocalypse is coming!! The end of the world is upon us!!" Eric shouts as they drag him across the grass, laughing in his face. The men shouldn't be laughing. By the next afternoon their worlds will end as they know them. The next afternoon the White House will come to the false conclusion that Yomi's drug is being injected intravenously, that the needle plunged into the maintenance man's belly had actually been meant for the president. They'll also make the correct assumption that the two are working together, and the hunt will be on.

That night, in the office of a Motel 6 on the outskirts of Washington D.C., when Eric asks the manager for two rooms as he always does, Yomi interrupts him.

"Actually, we'll share a room," she says, giving Eric's butt a quick squeeze, surprising him with a sudden friskiness that continues once they're in the room. Sex is Yomi's idea for a fitting celebration of their successful dosing of the White House well. At first Eric misjudges her cries of second-time pain for orgasmic squeals of pleasure. Afterwards, Yomi tells him how she's been calling herself a born-again-virgin for years, even though most people think it's a joke.

"You're not joking?" Eric asks. He's never heard of such a thing.

"No way," Yomi bubbles, jumping up to show him the blood stain on the sheets.

"My hymen regrew – my gynecologist confirmed it, told me it happens a lot when a woman doesn't have sex for many years – for me it's been almost twenty."

Eric shakes his head with disbelief.

"Twenty years of . . .nothing?"

Eric would hardly claim to be an expert on female masturbation tendencies. But from what his girlfriends have told him most single women engage in it on a regular basis. At least the normal ones do.

"That's right. Nothing."

Yomi's sure tone of voice portrays the pride she has in her sexual discipline, what she considers a key ingredient to her recent, long-awaited success.

"Are you normal?" Eric asks her, mostly kidding. But, like almost everything he says, she takes him seriously.

"No, I'm not normal. Why, are you?"

Eric pulls her back onto the bed.

"Yeah right – I should have been thrown into the loony bin more than just once by now."

"You've been thrown in once?"

"Oh yeah," Eric continues. "They caught me walking buck naked down the middle of a four-lane highway, headin' straight into the traffic with nothing but a sombrero coverin' up my balls . . ."

Yomi falls into his chest, giggling wildly.

"Tell me more!" she demands.

"Let's see - I'd just gotten back from Chiapas, where I was studying Mayan irrigation techniques – I think the sun got to me, the sun and all those pastel colors . . .not to mention the tequila."

Eric winds up rambling on for over an hour. Yomi lets him, making sure to say "Oh, really?" or "No way!" at all the right moments. By that point she'd caught enough glimpses of it to know that when Eric's ego rises up, a rare event, it shines with an unobtrusive sparkle, a light she only wants to get closer to. When his dramatic tale is over Yomi changes the subject by telling him about the lawn mower man she stabbed in the belly.

"I feel so bad," she laments.

"What's going to happen to him?"

"I don't know what a concentration that high will do – he'll probably die a strange death, squealing like a little girl while his balls shrivel up into raisins."

Eric winces.

"We can't kill anyone else, okay?" Yomi says, darkly playful.

"Okay."

That night, after the sex he'd been anticipating for months, after recounting his brush with mental illness, Eric comes to the decision that if Yomi isn't the one he's meant to spend his life with, at least he'll devote all of himself to the task of finding out. He doesn't ask her if she loves him. She couldn't have pronounced the word anyway.

Although their budget affords them the ability to sleep

in penthouse suites of the nicest downtown hotels, Eric's woodsy instincts usually guide them to an out-of-the-way backpacker hostel, a country bed & breakfast, or a tent pitched on the bank of some remote reservoir. Yomi, although naturally much less inclined towards rustic accommodations than her partner, preferring shiny bathrooms and room service, lets Eric control this one aspect of their operation. She recognizes the sacrifices he's making to help her. And, having held out on him physically for so long, Yomi is certain he made this commitment to her without any expectation of the physical rewards he's now receiving. So she keeps most of her discomforts to herself, learning to enjoy melting marshmallows over campfires, sleeping in rickety bunk beds, and peeing in outhouses.

Traveling frugally, they're able to devote most of their substantial budget to the logistics of not getting caught. They change outfits and disguises in every new city. They buy the best wigs and makeup and clothes they can find. In early morning dress-up sessions they help each other change race, profession, and sexual orientation. They switch cars in every new state, alter their accents from region to region. Eric, relishing the revival of his acting skills, goes over the top with some of his performances. In Memphis he dresses up as a clown and Yomi dons a business suit to personify his booking manager. Eric almost gets them caught when he breaks out into a random street performance downtown, violating city rules by performing without a permit even though his amateur clowning barely attracts a crowd. They have to run from the cops, evading capture by hiding out for a night underneath a dock on the muddy bank of the Mississippi.

Over the next six months, working their way around the United States with relative ease, Eric lets himself fall in love, slowly and gradually, on pace with the seasons. His love attaches to specific views of Yomi, things he focuses his attention on for long moments of time, like the smooth slope of her neck while she rests against the window of their vehicle watching the scenery go by. Or the curve of her brown cheek against the sky when he kisses the spot between her nose and the corner of her mouth. And, eventually, the back of her round head while she falls asleep curled into him. His love accumulates in these tiny, daily pieces. Spontaneous kisses, bites of food passed back and forth, and playful smiles all add up to the kind of love Eric has always fantasized about, a love with the possibility of permanence.

In the White House media conference room the major networks brief the president on the lead story of that night's evening news broadcast, something that's become a daily ritual of late. The CBS representative opens the discussions.

"That NPR man broke the story before we knew what was happening, and we're sorry about that, Mr. President – but we've all met and decided to sweep Mr. Jones' . . .outburst, so to speak, under the rug – tonight, with the help of a few cooperating doctors, we plan to break a story introducing the new disease we'll tentatively be calling Adult Male Lethargy Syndrome, to be described as a combination of depression and adult attention deficit syndrome. We'll announce that cases are popping up by the hundreds of thousands along the East Coast. We'll say the methods of contracting it are unknown, and that the disease is expected to sweep across the nation. How does that sound, Mr. President, sir?"

The media representatives hang on his answer.

"Fine, I guess – but won't people get paranoid and start to panic?"

"That's where you step in, sir," the NBC man says. "That's when one of your agencies nails these two crazy scientists. We say your people have come up with a 'vaccine' to AMLS and bam, you save the men of this country from . . .humiliation and disgrace. Then you spend a few hundred million on finding a 'cure' for the ones that have already ingested the drug."

The president nods slowly. He glances over his shoulder at the head of the CIA, who shuffles his feet and looks down at the ground.

"You are close to getting these scientists, correct?" NBC asks.

"Actually, we lost them in the Smoky Mountains," the president says, his voice thin and weak. "They just vanished off the screen," he continues, pausing to gulp down the rest of his water from a glass on the podium.

"So, what do you want the White House position to be tonight, on the discovery of the disease?"

"That our nation's best scientists are hard at work on a vaccine and should have one ready very soon. And that we are close to apprehending those responsible for this national catastrophe."

"We can't say the last part," the NBC man says.

"Why not?"

"Because, you're not close – they've vanished from your radar screen – so we just have to play dumb," he continues. "Sometimes it's the only thing we can do."

"Okay."

Playing dumb is one thing this president is good at. He should have been an actor, like his father's pal Ronald. He could still be having fun blowing lines and partying with rock stars instead of being burdened by such an important job. The president begins to nod off into sleep.

"I think I need a nap," he says, just before his head falls onto the table, stunning the room into silence.

The secret service chief standing by the door closes his eyes. His face squeezes tight with the pain of failure. The president has obviously been dosed. His men shuffle about anxiously, unsure of what to do. They will all be fired by the end of the day. By the end of the day, the White House will question its theories on the scientists' method of delivering their drug.

The president's bedroom in the White House is all flowers and fluff. His father's wife, the first lady a few terms back, had it redesigned in a classic style popular with homemaking women in the 1950's. The president routinely spends very little waking time in the stuffy room. But the day after his meeting with the press about the AMLS story he sleeps through the morning, his body shocked into submission by the sudden change in hormone production. He finally rises around noon, after sleeping fourteen straight hours, and announces that it's time for the family to head out to the ranch house in Kansas. One of his top aides speaks against this idea.

"But, sir, you are of course aware that the members of the Alliance are coming here tomorrow for an emergency meeting to address the urgent need to apprehend the two scientists that are - "

"I don't care, really – I need to rest, to just be with my wife and the kids on the ranch . . .you know what I mean, Joe – you're a family man, right?"

The aide nods quickly. Along with his fellow advisors, all of them recently drugged by the White House water, he's eager to be home as well, to be sprawled out on a couch or bed letting the world go by, a behavior that's proving to be the most common initial reaction to Yomi's drug.

"No problem, sir. I understand completely."

"Good."

By nightfall the president's family, his wife Beth-Ann and their three children, are gathered on the carpeted floor of the ranch's sprawling living den playing rummy. The president, having removed the game animal heads from the conference room walls shortly after their arrival, is already feeling better about things. Change is in the air. He can feel it. They take a break in the game and he cooks dinner. When he dozes off in his chair, the kids ask their mother what's wrong with dad. He's never cooked anything for them before.

"You're father is sick, that's all," Beth-Ann says, trying to keep the worry out of her voice.

"With what?" asks Sam, the oldest of the three.

"I don't know," Beth-Ann answers, too tired to make up an answer for her children.

Leaving her husband asleep in the chair, once her children are quiet in their rooms upstairs Beth-Ann settles in to watch an interview taped earlier that day of Hillary Clinton, making her first public appearance since literally disappearing from American politics a few months before. Beth-Ann brings a pint of Ben & Jerry's Cherry Garcia ice cream into the billowing folds of their bed to help her get through the recording. She never misses watching Mrs. Clinton whenever the former First Lady appears on television.

It's her addiction, fetish, and jealous obsession all rolled into one. Beth-Ann's hands shake as she pushes play on the DVD player. The interview, conducted by Rupert Jones, takes place in a dimly lit room with rock walls and black padded yoga mats on the floor. The geographic location is confidential. Beth-Ann sits cross-legged at the foot of the bed, gorging herself on the ice cream, pausing the recording during close-ups on Hillary's face, rewinding it at times to replay her particularly eloquent statements. Always popular and with hordes of friends, Beth-Ann had never felt inferior to any woman until Hillary Clinton became president of a whole country. She's ever aware that she married into her political position by capturing the eyes of an oil baron's wild son so many years ago, and knows that she'll never be elected as the leader of anything more than a too-serious church group or a too-pretentious women's group. Beth-Ann tosses the empty pint to the floor and turns up the volume on the television. Now well into the interview, Hillary begins speaking with exuberant passion.

"The citizens of New America believe in a new kind of world, one in which women are the leaders, the foundation of society and the makers of history, as they have been in many traditional cultures since time immemorial . . .we believe women will lead humanity into the future, guided by intuition."

"Well, you certainly are a symbol of this belief – being elected president of your new nation," Jones comments.

When the brazen young reporter asks Hillary if she has anything to say about a pair of renegade scientists somehow crippling the male population of the East Coast, Hillary can't hide a slight glint in the corner of an eye.

"I have to say it's about time."

"Me too," Rupert says. "As long as they steer clear of me," he adds, chuckling.

Beth-Ann pauses the recording. She needs a break from watching this superwoman say another word. And maybe she needs more sweets, like cookies or chocolate this time.

Mark Reynolds, now unemployed lawyer and stay-at-home dad, is out in his backyard teaching his boys how to make fire. Like millions of men his age now infected with AMLS, Mark has taken up a passionate interest in primitive survival skills. He and his boys have built shelters, carved bows and arrows, and foraged for wild edibles in the empty lot next door. Now his kids are gathered around him as he spins a hand drill made of a dried mullen stalk into a block of pine. The children watch eagerly as black ash builds up and spills out the notch he's cut into the board. Strands of smoke begin wafting up as his drilling intensifies. Just as he's about to give up, the excited shouts of his boys urging him on, a pulsating red coal drops out of the ash pile. He picks it up and places it into a bundle of leaves and birch bark. Cupping the ball of tinder in his hands he blows into its center until flames rise up. He tosses the flaming bundle beneath the teepee of sticks he's arranged, and soon a campfire is raging. The delighted boys take in their father, a man who can make fire, with wide eyes and a new awe. Sara shouts down to him from the kitchen window.

"Honey, I think you should come and take a look at this!"

Mark pretends not to hear her. He doesn't want to leave the fire. He and his boys are huddled around it, adding sticks and dry leaves, enthralled by the flames.

"Mark!?" Sara yells again, walking out across the back deck to stare down at the scene below. She shakes her head – her backyard looks like the set for some suburban Survivor episode.

"Dear, please – can you just come inside for a minute? You don't even have to clean your feet off this time."

Mark goes barefoot during his afternoons in the backyard. These afternoons extend into evenings so often that Sara has threatened to stop cooking dinner. She always makes him wash the black bottoms of his feet with the hose outside, a chore Mark finds pointless and painful. Torn between maintaining domestic harmony and satisfying his recently awakened primitive psyche, he reluctantly leaves his protesting boys with the fire and walks towards the house. When he steps up onto the deck Sara kisses him. His lips are unresponsive.

Inside he takes a seat at the marble counter while his wife turns up the volume of their tiny television set. The lead story is almost over.

"The victims of Adult Male Lethargy Syndrome now number in the millions," the reporter announces as she stands outside a government laboratory in Los Alamos, where a vaccine to the disease is supposedly being worked on. "In addition," the reporter continues, "the President has promised the nation that the scientists here in Los Alamos will now focus their efforts on coming up with a cure for those already afflicted with the disease."

"See, honey, this is what you must have," Sara says.

"Lethargy syndrome? But I'm not lethargic . . ." Mark protests. A colored graphic comes up on the screen displaying a list of the condition's major symptoms. The reporter reads them out. Sara nods along with every one.

"Number one – loss of all sexual desire. Two – loss of all professional responsibility. Three – indifference to money. Number four – childlike behavior and mindset. And, finally, number five – a complete inability to make important, serious decisions."

"See, you have every one of these!" Sara exclaims, lowering the volume on the television.

"Yeah, but . . .most of them aren't that bad, really, except for the first one, I guess. I'm really sorry about that . . .I don't know what's going on down there."

He nods down at his crotch, then back up at her.

"But, otherwise, I'm happy as a lark."

"Well, I'm miserable as a magpie, and we're about to be bankrupt. Do you even know what bankrupt means, Mark?"

She storms out of the room, leaving Mark at the counter, shirtless and barefoot and covered in soot. After a moment spent pondering the word bankrupt and coming up empty, his mind wanders to more important matters. He slips out the back door and down the stairs of the deck, heading for the fire, eager to let the sound of crackling wood and the smell of smoke take him back to the place he's starting to remember. This place feels like the sunrise, like sharp morning light striking wet stones on a wilderness beach. It's a place that feels like the top of a mountain on a clear, cold January night, when the stars are more abundant than darkness, casting the light of a full moon. It's the smell of evergreens and mist, mud and rotting leaves, saltwater and rain and sand. Every moment in this place is defined by the immediacy of survival, by fire and food, shelter and warmth. This place our ancestors knew intimately, a place that has been forgotten one century at a time to become a distant memory stumbled on in the occasional dream. Even the map that might have taken us back there has been forgotten. But although these dosed men are given the gift of living in this primal, timeless land, the reality is that they're wanderers lost in evolutionary purgatory, born-again cavemen caught in Suburbia, by no means an enviable state of being.

"Nothing is holy . . . everything is sacred."

- Mantra carved into the wall of
Eric Underwood's log cabin.

Welcomed into New America by the open arms of its citizens and its leaders alike, Yomi and Eric are given their own underground house to live in. It's a place to hide out after completing their dosing of the United States, a haven to collect themselves and figure out what to do next. At first Yomi even settles into a domestic routine of sorts, sweeping and dusting, spending most of her time homemaking, surprising Eric on a daily basis. But as their relationship settles into the earth along with their home she quickly grows bored. Her scientist's mind craves the stimulation of the lab to the point where she can't let her body fully surrender to the warm comfort of domestic satisfaction. So Yomi applies for and receives a budget from the Experience Committee to begin construction of a laboratory adjacent to their dwelling, a project she dives into with most of her energy.

At first Eric hardly notices his abandonment. Spending his days alone exploring, he thinks he'll never grow tired of the landscape. The country has temporarily closed its boundaries even though the underground dwellings take up only one percent of the available land space. Everyone settles down into what they do best. Musicians collaborate and form new bands. Actors and filmmakers set up a movie studio and start shooting films. Businessmen meet with environmentalists to brainstorm about clean technologies. With a constitutional ban on the use of fossil fuels, combined with a location in an area isolated from the developed world, New America is blessed with its own micro climate. Eric notices intense shades of greens and blues through the clear air. The wind tastes fresh and is loaded with oxygen, imbuing the locals with a constant supply of natural energy. Eric watches the stars give nightly performances, their brilliance uncontested thanks to the curfew on the use of artificial lights after nightfall. He sees magic revealed on a daily basis, like Bob Dylan, all white hair and wrinkles, reliving his youth by playing his old acoustic songs in coffee shop caves and teahouses in the trees. He attends Bill Clinton's monthly speeches on the economics of intellect and the purpose of passion. He listens to Robin Williams serve up nightly, fifteen-minute comedy bits in the grand dining hall to lift any moods that may be sinking. Talent and genius combine in spontaneous bursts of creation. With so much beauty around him Eric, along with most everyone living in New America, has the unspoken feeling that it's all too good to be true.

As Yomi immerses herself even deeper into her lab, staying locked inside for days at a time, Eric feels the need to distance himself from his immediate surroundings. So he starts making overnight forays by horseback up into the Selkirk Mountains, where he locates the myriad sources of the Goldstream River, which flows through the heart of New America's territory. Although he loves getting to know the river and its tributaries, the number of trout and salmon in any one stretch, the sharp dappling of sunlight on the water's surface, he continually longs for the calm lakes and ponds of upstate New York. He misses the dark suspension, the womb-like peace of hovering in his private, murky depths. Out on the wide-open plains it seems impossible to go unnoticed by something or someone. Eric can't stand this state of constant visibility. He begins to wonder if perhaps he's just shy. He brings this concern up with Yomi one night after they've returned from dinner in the communal dining room.

"Aren't I just an introverted weirdo? I mean, who likes hanging out with diving beetles instead of with other people?" he asks her as they lay in their great bed tucked into an exposed curve of jagged bedrock.

"If you're a weirdo than I am too," Yomi says, grinning. "I've told you how I'd rather spend a weekend night with my chimps than with any people I know . . . until I met you, my big crawdad!"

"Thanks. I'm not sure that's a compliment, though."

"To be a crawdad?"

"No – I've told you that I'd love to be reincarnated as a crayfish any day – I was talking about how you implied that I'm merely better company than a chimpanzee . . ."

"Oh, but that's a compliment too! You haven't even met my chimps yet. They're total characters, every one of them – intelligent, caring, and resourceful – everything you are!"

Eric winces with a sharp yearning for the aqueous worlds of Upstate New York.

"I'm so excited that they're coming here soon, to live in my new lab," Yomi continues.

"Yeah, that's great."

Eric rolls over on his side. He's having trouble being happy for her. This is why it might be better to live alone, he thinks, at least on the whole. As much as he hates loneliness, it still beats the peculiar domestic isolation he's been feeling lately. Yomi cocks her head. She can sense his emotional retreat.

"What's wrong?"

"It's not like I can just build myself a lake to study out here," he complains.

"Why can't you?"

He rolls back over to face her. Yomi sits up while she speaks.

"C'mon, these people have more money than god – and they love us – they'll do anything you want. Trust me."

"They do have some really big bulldozers . . ."

Yomi climbs on top of him, slides one hand down his pants, and clicks out the light with the other.

"They sure do," she whispers in her seductive, motel room voice, a voice Eric has been hearing less and less of these days.

Later, after sex, after Eric has drifted off to sleep beneath the pages of his magazine, Yomi slips out of bed to feed her craving for test tubes, sterile steel, and the seductive precision of her first lover. Her secret goal, her new affair, is to convert the liquid drug into a gas.

As warm spring breezes turn the prolific grasses from rusting brown to golden green, Yomi and Eric are united as husband and wife in a subdued, Buddhist style wedding. Their honeymoon is an overnight on the island Eric had built out in the middle of his man-made lake. They make love for hours with the stars for a blanket. Afterwards, they cuddle and discuss the future.

"We could just stay here you know," Eric says.

"Why do you keep saying things like that?" Yomi fires back, propping herself up on an elbow. "Our project is what I'm supposed to be doing with my life, Eric, and I thought you supported that. I thought you l-uff-oved me."

Eric furrows his brow at the persistence of her impediment. He'd been under the impression that true love, and making a home, would cure her problem with saying the L word.

"I do, it's just, I mean, maybe what we're doing will only cause more harm in the end, mess up the balance of things. You know?"

"No, I don't know," Yomi stammers. "We are changing the world for the better. Trust me. It's time for women to take over, which is something we can make possible, something that's been l-uff-ong overdue – goddamnit I can't even talk!"

"Whatever you say, Doctor," Eric says, pulling her torso down to meet his, rolling over on top of her, eager for the soft mindlessness of skin on skin.

A few days after returning from their island honeymoon, Yomi visits Hillary's private dwelling. Although she remains his wife, friend, and occasional lover, Mrs. Clinton refuses to live with her husband, claiming she needs to sleep alone on most nights in order to keep her intuition in tune with her dreams. Her entranceway is adorned with freshly cut flowers and colored mesh butterflies hanging from transparent fishing line. Yomi knocks on the recycled plastic door with firm confidence.

"Come in," shouts the former first lady. The door opens and Yomi steps in. Hillary, in the midst of a sun salutation on her yoga mat, smiles over a spandex-clad kneecap.

"Look at you, Doctor!"

"What?" Yomi says, slipping over to sit at a carved wooden dining table off to one side of the expansive room. Hillary undoes herself from the downward dog to sit with her legs crossed on the mat.

"You're so . . .glowing, that's all. I guess that means the honeymoon went well?"

"It did, thank you," Yomi says, feeling herself blush. She looks away from the only woman she's ever been intimidated by.

"The stars were . . .I can't say, not in words, anyway."

"I know exactly what you mean. Bill and I spent a night camping out in the fields . . .the night skies are absolutely incredible up here . . .But there's hardly much time for stargazing these days."

"No, there isn't," Yomi agrees, meeting her eyes for the first time. Hillary wrinkles her brow and stands up.

"You seem content and restless at the same time, Dr. Nguyen."

"I am," Yomi admits. "Part of me could just surrender to how it feels to be here, to be in Eric's arms – that part says forget about my crazy dream, because it will only get me in trouble anyway. Or, worse, get the whole world in trouble. But . . ."

"But you can't forget it, can you?"

Hillary lays a hand down on Yomi's small shoulder. The scientist shakes her head.

"I want to dose the rest of the world," Yomi states with characteristic bluntness.

"Well, this country wants to keep helping you," President Clinton says. "We want to make it easy for the two of you to finish the job you started. Every worthwhile job deserves to be finished, at least in my book."

Hillary takes a seat across from Yomi at the hand-carved table.

"We're becoming a very powerful nation now, Doctor Nguyen. And you are our hero."

"I am?"

Yomi doesn't want to be a hero. But she has to admit it feels good, like a rush, like sex.

"I've turned my drug into a gas," she announces, her eyes lighting up with the excitement of her new accomplishment.

"Oh yeah?" Hillary asks.

"Yeah."

Hillary smiles. She wants to reach out and touch the intensity in Yomi's wide pupils. Instead she takes the scientist's hand and squeezes it tight.

With the guidance and financial backing of New America, as summer sets in the husband-and-wife team heads back out to continue their mission of subduing the world's male population. Their multi-million dollar budget and web of connections are poised to shuttle them around the continents in total secrecy like a global, Underground Railroad for two. The couple's sex life takes off as they shed most of the monogamous monotony that had begun to threaten the confines of their underground house in British Columbia. Back out on the road together, beginning in Europe with a plan to move west to east, they soil the sheets of hostel rooms and drink the local beer after hard days of good work. Yomi hones her skills in bed so well that Eric remains in disbelief of the almost blank slate of her sexual history. But in the midst of this return to romantic bliss, tugging Eric down from the glorious heights of purpose and passion, are new doubts. He realizes that spending so much time assisting Yomi accomplish her dream has taken him away from his own higher aspirations.

At the age of seventeen Eric had a vision of his ultimate purpose in life. It happened on hallucinogenic mushrooms, while camping with his girlfriend during his junior year of high school. They'd pitched a tent on a tiny island in the middle of a wilderness pond in the Adirondacks, where they'd caught fish all day long and cooked them over a campfire. Then the 'shroom tea kicked in and Eric fell flat on his back. The stars rained down on him. Loons howled in three-dimensional echoes like a chorus of lunatics screaming the call of the wild. Eric closed his eyes and watched the evolution of mankind unfold across the picture screen of his mind. By the time he opened them back up his body had slithered its way down the sloping rock shore of the island. The top of his head dipped into the water. His thoughts, his ego, his entire self spilled out of his head and into the lake. United with water, one with H20 molecules, Eric closed his eyes again. This time he saw into the future, from the perspective of water itself. He could see a black hole of consumption, a scorching sun converting every last drop into vapor, the last remaining pools of water slipping haplessly into the burning atmosphere. By this time there are no more people. Bugs are thriving, but even they have to begin fighting for sporadic drops of the life-sustaining liquid. When Eric finally woke up from the trip, regurgitating lake water and feeling the concerned arms of his girlfriend draped around his shoulders, he decided to make saving fresh water his life's mission. Now, as Yomi's dedicated accomplice, he is suddenly filled with heavy regret from the fear that he's stepped off this path. But his first commitment to her, before the promise of marriage, is to help her until the goal of dosing two billion men has been reached. Eric vows to himself he will stick this part out. The vow of marriage, however, will be a separate challenge. Yomi's true love will always be science. He knows this as well as she does.

On the road Eric has another vision. It happens in Venice, where they splurge on a four-star room in the Colombina Hotel to rest after the complicated job of dosing the city of canals. Maybe it happens because Venice is arguably the most romantic place in the world. But it's likely due to all the water, water underneath their hotel room, dark canal water flowing constantly all around them, the amniotic fluid of a great civilization fed by criss-crossing veins of ancient water contained within stone and concrete. The vision happens on a full moon night in their room in the Colombina. Moonlight refracts off the moving canal below, in through the wooden paned windows to splash across Yomi's brown skin contorting beneath him. For a moment her belly is bathed in a lunar spotlight. Eric, moving in a slow rhythm inside her, back and forth above her, wishes she wasn't on birth control, silently cursing the six-month injection that ensures his seed won't take root. He can feel his entire being, each and every cell in his body futilely pushing for one sperm to reach a nonexistent egg. Afterwards, lying beside her with the windows open, they listen together to the constant swish of the canal.

"Let's have a baby," Eric blurts into the sex-infused air. The statement gives him a rush of adrenaline. His skin tingles with excitement.

"I'm not ready."

"Why not?"

Eric sits up with the question. Yomi curls into ball.

"I still have too much to do."

"More science, you mean?"

Eric swings his legs down off the bed. Waiting for an answer he stares straight into the beam of moonlight.

"Yes. More science."

Eric stares into the moon.

Eric Underwood's urge to reproduce refuses to fade. He visualizes his babies crawling about their rock-walled dwelling tucked into the earth. He thinks often about the comfort in the feeling of their home, the warmth of all the great, inspired people surrounding them in New America. His body remembers the nourishment of communal dinners made using food grown twenty yards from the dining hall. He feels his clock ticking, every minute building up to some impending alarm, a siren that, being a man, he never thought he even possessed. He'd always assumed that women were the ones with the baby clocks. But the woman he happened to have married, even though she's approaching the end of her reproductive years, seems to have been constructed without the alarm feature. Or maybe Eric is just hearing the ticking in Yomi that she herself grew deaf to long ago, her womanly urges repressed since high school, when she began sacrificing the feeling of happiness in favor of the all out pursuit of her dream. They both know that what they're attempting to accomplish will, if successful, alter the course of human history forever. Together they will live on for millennia, in literature and history classes, in bar and café discussions. They'll be cited in poetry and mythologized by new religions. Yomi doesn't seem to care about this potential immortality. She's driven only by purpose. But Eric can't help worrying that maybe, blinded by the intensity of her dream, she risks never experiencing some of the best things living has to offer, simple things, like the daily joys of family.

What Eric doesn't know is that Yomi is aware of the possibility that she might miss out on this side of life. She's acknowledged this exact possibility for decades. He is also unaware that she's created a gaseous version of her testosterone inhibitor, something she's brought along for their journey around the world.

Juan Franco, eighteen, has just completed his training to become a *mama.* In a sacred village uninhabited except during these initiation rituals, tucked by a rushing stream deep within the jungle, he's approached by the Water Carrier, the eldest, most revered priest of the group, who's just returned from eight days of praying on the mountaintop with the other *mamas.* In a rehearsed gesture the elder offers Juan the special gourd made of hollow stone that has hung around his neck for more than fifty years, what holds part of the first drop of water ever to fall on *Gonawindua* mountain, a tiny pool he's just replenished, water to be used in the ceremonies and rituals over the upcoming year. Speaking without talking, the elder informs Juan how he's been chosen by the spirits to be the next Water Carrier, to wear the stone gourd and make the yearly pilgrimages to the spring, a source that is becoming harder and harder to find as the water flows less and less. On his first trip to the sacred spring, the elder Water Carrier declares, Juan will be taking an American priest and her husband, two Younger Brothers that have been invited to help the *mamas* with their prayers on the mountaintop.

Ben and Maria spend their first night in Colombia in Santa Marta, a quiet city on the Caribbean Coast, the laid-back beach retreat of Colombians, who leave Cartagena to the tourists. After saying her nightly prayers of thankfulness Maria falls right asleep in their room tucked into the side street hostel. Ben tosses and turns all night long, reading Dickens by candlelight in an attempt to recreate the feeling of home in the strange surroundings. He can't avoid the fact that the air feels so different to his skin. He wonders what kind of crazy dreams the salt-infused, tropical air might inspire. As dawn licks the windowsill Ben tries to focus on the sound of his wife's rhythmic breathing. Her calm inhales and exhales become a metronome in tune with his heart, finally lulling him into something close to sleep.

After their breakfast in the plant-filled courtyard and an easy conversation with the hostel owners, a pleasant German couple who declare Colombia to be the most magical country in the world, a place they never want to leave, there is a ring at the front door. The owners rise and let in Danilo, the man the Kogi elders have chosen to be the liaison between their primitive, isolated villages and the modern world. Danilo has a warm nature and an easy smile, two traits that more than make up for his ragged English. He helps load Ben and Maria into his jeep and they roll out of town, through numerous military checkpoints, until they're bouncing up mud-rutted roads through the jungle. *Nabusimake* is a cluster of thatched, peaked-roof huts, each with two wooden poles on top representing the dual forces of nature, the black-and-white dichotomy of creation. The village, empty except during a few days every month when the people converge there for ceremonies and festivals, is set on a plateau about halfway up the rising range of the Sierra Nevada. Upon their arrival everyone gathers in a large half circle to greet them -the *mamas* in their long white shirts and pointed hats, naked children, women in white skirts woven from *agave,* farmers with sun-darkened skin and dirt-caked hands. After being introduced by Danilo the *mamas* greet the couple one at a time, speaking volumes in their eyes while their mouths stay closed. Maria and Ben can almost feel the wisdom spilling out of these men, essential truths they've all discovered along the course of their eighteen years of training and beyond. After the *mamas* depart to their own cluster of huts to prepare for the week-long journey with the outsiders, set to begin the following morning, the village children gather on an outdoor stage, where they sing and dance the traditional songs in a performance dedicated to the two guests. Later, after a feast of local harvests, roasted monkey and shellfish and fresh mangoes, Danilo escorts the couple to the town's guest hut, built in the local style of bamboo walls and a grass thatch roof. Hanging candles and ocean artifacts decorate the interior. But even after all the warmth of their welcoming party Ben is still having trouble settling down. He paces the packed earth floor of their one-room hut.

"What's wrong with me?" he asks his wife. "I don't want to be anywhere but home, where it feels right – we're such outsiders here – what are we doing, anyway?"

Maria continues her recent trend of being direct with her husband. Her tone borders on harsh.

"You can't live through your books forever, Ben. It's a big world, a world we're obligated to engage in every day, on the deepest level possible. That's my belief, and I know it's yours too. Al is being taken care of, our house and fields and forests aren't going anywhere."

"I know . . ."

Ben stops pacing and kicks at the dirt floor.

"And we have something very important to do here. These people are going out on a serious limb by inviting me – an outsider and a woman – to help them pray. They're taking as much of a leap as we are."

"I know, I know . . .it's just . . ."

"It's just what?"

"Don't get me wrong - I want the earth to survive, and I believe prayer could be a means to that end - but maybe what we're doing back in Vermont is more beneficial to this goal than anything we can do here. Maybe our survival, yours and mine, I mean, has to come first – lead by example they say, right?"

Maria does not reply. The same sort of idea has been secretly plaguing her subconscious ever since their arrival in Colombia, a place they could never be anything but outsiders. Once a few hours into their trek the next morning, in fact, it will be Maria pushing for them to retreat back home to the familiar. Ben, awakening to a new side of his self, will urge them to press on.

Juan, making his first journey to the ancestral source, and the former Water Carrier, on his final trip to the holy spring, lead the American couple in the three-day trek up *Gonawindua*. Danilo accompanies the party as a translator. To Juan the white woman priest seems hardly present, hiding from the intensity of the setting through her husband. Juan can hear Ben's thoughts, and knows the westerner is catching more and more snapshots of what he's thinking as the hike continues. Telepathy is a skill the *mamas* and many other Elder Brothers acquire easily, the way two lifelong friends will sometimes think the same thought simultaneously. Younger Brothers like Ben and Maria are not known to have this ability. Juan understands the white man is occupied by taking care of his wife, and knows Maria is pregnant before she does. He can see her spirit distracted by the new life inside her, a reality that's affecting her experience of everything.

While trekking up the mountain the visitors slip into other realms of space, time, and thought. The air is misty, green vipers dangle from green branches, thunderstorms and rainbows define the afternoons. While taking in the sights and smells and sounds of the world being born all over again every day, every hour, Ben and Maria begin to understand how these mountains could be viewed as the Heart of the Earth. They have intense dreams in the night, and wake up reaching for something to hold onto in the darkness of their canvas tents. Holding onto each other, they aren't saying much, both engrossed in the effects the exotic surroundings are having on their interior landscapes.

Away from home Ben is coming to the same certain conclusion Eric Underwood is arriving at on the opposite side of the globe – it's time to have a child. He knows that the world he and Maria have created in Vermont is the perfect, magical place to bring children into, safe from the cyber-addicted culture of America, far from malls and fast-food joints, a place where their kids will be left alone to discover life on its own terms. Even though this call is mingling with parrot shrieks and monkey howls, Ben hears it very clearly, because he's ready to hear it. Having put aside his books and his cooking for a few weeks, his senses open to the whispers he's been ignoring for years while waiting for the right opportunity to be the kind of father his own dad never became. His father's absence, the nights of whiskey and poker that grew into years of whiskey and gutters, an absence that wasn't always physical but always present, is what originally sparked his intense desire not only to be a good parent, but a true father in every facet of the word. In pursuit of this dream Ben has devoted the last ten years of his life to making it possible for him to be a full-time dad, to make the job of fatherhood his career. Although he won't know it until after they return home, after the ultrasounds and blood work, his career as a father has already started.

Without the moorings of her pulpit in the church or her cozy spots in their log house, in the jungle Maria finds herself needing Ben's grounding effect more than ever. She stays close to him on the trail, by his side around the camps, curled into him all night long inside their tent. Perpetually open to the spirit world, Maria wonders why for once in her life she is deaf and blind to this other dimension of reality. New England ghosts she can understand. They're mostly farmers clinging to their fields, or mothers hanging on to their hearths. She even enjoys their company at times. But the entities of creation surrounding her here in these tropical mountains, mysterious and invisible and speaking in languages she'll never understand, are another story. Back home the sacred sustains her, lifting her above the mundane. In the Sierra Nevada she drifts helplessly amidst spirits she can't see, forced to let the *mamas* lead while she focuses on her feet striking the soft, damp trail one step after another, day after day.

After three days of walking through the damp jungles they finally reach the high altitude spring. There, seated on a cluster of moss-covered rocks, Juan Franco works hard at directing his mind towards the task ahead. He focuses on the hairs covering his arms, seeing them as the plants and trees they symbolize. His skin becomes the soil, the blood in his veins the myriad streams flowing underground. Trying hard to focus, he can feel the eyes of the elder and the foreigners heavy on him. His insides jitter with unfamiliar nerves. He makes a point not to show these nerves as he sings the right songs and makes the right coca leaf offerings. He sinks the stone gourd into the bubbling spring, replenishing the original water of life, a supply for the new year of ceremonies. Juan can't help his hands from shaking slightly from the enormity of the task at hand. This water is the core of what sustains the *mamas'* work. As part of the closing ceremony, Juan passes his coca gourd around, much larger than the Water Carrier gourd and made of wood instead of stone. According to tradition, being a woman Maria does not partake in the coca. When the gourd is offered to Ben he hesitates for a moment before plunging in the pestle and lifting a clump of mashed leaves into his mouth.

After the spring it's a short climb to the mountaintop, where the American couple joins the circle of priests. They emulate the cross-legged positions of the *mamas*, palms draped over kneecaps, eyes closed. The giant boulder making up the summit is smooth, worn down from centuries of similar gatherings. Below them the jungle stretches out towards both horizons in waves of lime green, terminating only in the turquoise blue of the Caribbean to the north. As the day progresses the *mamas* strain with the effort of praying. Their faces squeeze tight with tension as they build a prayer in the circle of space between them, humming a slow song one drawn-out word at a time. Maria, usually adept at seeing elements of the spirit world, relies on Ben's whispered descriptions of what's taking place. Ben watches the air change in the middle of the circle, sees it thicken into an almost gelatinous texture, and whispers what he's seeing to his wife. Soon a physical ball of prayer energy swells up, with a texture he thinks he could feel if he dared to walk out and touch it. As hours pass the ball swells larger and larger, lifting above the stone summit and the wooden bowl of burning coca leaves. The *mamas'* heads tilt back in minute increments, the globe of energy rising at the same pace, connected to their foreheads by invisible strands of intention. Ben, sucking on the clump of pungent leaves, uses the swell of energy it creates to pray in much the same way he does in Maria's church, except this time he knows his prayers are actually going somewhere, having an influence on something. He can feel a chord of focused thought extending from his forehead, feeding the ball of prayers. As day becomes night their bodies convulse with the strain of the job. The song builds into a cacophony of intertwining voices as their communal prayer, now a shimmering orb competing with the stars, lifts up and away, detaching itself from the minds that created it, splintering into filaments of energy and shooting out to course around the world.

By the time dawn is approaching the coca leaves have stopped burning. The *mamas* use their white cloaks for blankets, curling up in the same spots they've been praying in. A couple hours later they'll wake up and do it all over again. For centuries, they would only spend one such day on the mountaintop. Last year, after a week of trying to build prayers big enough to tip the scales of the planet's ecological balance, the *mamas* still didn't feel like they'd made enough of a difference. This year they've scheduled ten days on *Gonawindua*. That morning, with Danilo translating, the *mamas* tell Ben and Maria the problem, how the prayer they built in one day used to be enough, but now they need to construct one so much bigger to make any kind of impact. They can't rush the training of new *mamas*, but the seven of them won't be able to build a prayer any bigger without causing physical damage to their bodies. They ask Maria for her advice. She has a simple answer.

"You need a building to pray in," she advises them, speaking through Danilo. "You need a roof and walls to contain the prayers you make – instead of giving it away at night you could save them for a period of days or even months, building the prayer bigger each day, making it large enough to have an impact out there in the world, whatever that impact is supposed to be. That's what we do in our church, anyway."

In her Brattleboro church Maria watches prayers build up over time before bursting out the front doors during special services like Easter or Christmas Eve. As far as she knows, no one else in the congregation has ever witnessed these balls of energy collecting in the rafters above her pulpit. Upon hearing Danilo's translation of her advice the *mamas* nod and exchange glances as they consider her suggestion without speaking. Maria, exhausted by the effort of expressing her idea, overwhelmed by the group of spiritually powerful men surrounding her, has to back out of the circle to avoid fainting.

At the end of a week, after another three-day hike down from the mountain, the many shades of green finally give way to open sky and the huts in the village clearing. After returning to *Nabusimake,* surrounded by other women, Maria realizes she's pregnant. Then her frustrated desire to know these exotic spirits dissolves immediately into the all-encompassing humidity, and all she wants to do is go home.

Sara Reynolds didn't marry the most successful lawyer in Manhattan to be applying for a job, what she's just finished doing at their kitchen counter. Sara didn't marry for money, either, but all of a sudden they're running out of it. Their high society life has been eating through their savings at a rapid pace ever since her husband stopped working. As a shy, conservative bachelor, Mark had charmed her with the regimen of his routine, with his professionalism, honor, and dedication to his career. But now they have two boys, the public schools are a mess, and the burden of college tuitions will be upon them before they know it. Sara closes the classified section of the local paper on top of her welfare application. She presses her thumbs into her temples, hoping to ease the tightening of her scalp as Mark and their boys file in from their afternoon survivalist session in the backyard. The boys glance at the un-set table, then at the stovetop. They notice how nothing is cooking away like there usually is at this time of day.

"What's for dinner, mommy?"

"Yeah, mom?"

"Nothing," Sara says, snapping the word at them. The boys look up at their father, their new best friend, with a combination of disbelief and worry in their faces.

"Why don't you guys head upstairs for a bit," Mark says, shuttling them towards the stairs. "I'll take care of dinner," he adds. Returning to the counter he drapes an arm around his wife's shoulders.

"What's going on Sara?" Mark asks, nodding at the paper.

"What's going on is . . .I'm looking for a job."

"Oh. Why?"

She lifts her tear-streaked face and turns toward him.

"Why!? Are you really asking me that? Someone has to bring home some money, Mark, or we're going to lose everything, all of this – our entire life for Christ's sake!"

She waves her arms at the surroundings. Mark wrinkles his forehead.

"Will we lose the backyard?" he asks.

"Probably."

Mark winces. Sara releases a violent gush of air as she stands up.

"What about the boys, Sara? Are we going to lose the bo - "

"No, Mark, not the boys," she says quickly, before his face tightens up with any more fear.

"Well, things can't be that bad, then, if we still have the boys . . .but the backyard?"

Sara is furious at the glazed-over passivity in her husband's eyes, eyes that remind her of the spaced out hippies that had always surrounded her in college. She slaps him hard on the cheek. He recoils, stunned.

"What was that for?"

"I wanted to wake you up – to snap you out of . . .this!!"

She lifts her palms at him. Then she stands up, collects the classifieds in her arms, and marches out the front door, striding with purpose. Mark is left shaking his head in the kitchen, futilely pondering the concept of money.

Sara drives the manicured suburban streets, past all the perfect houses with their manicured, perfect lawns. The streets are completely empty. Usually at this time of day Sara is waving to a different friend along practically every block. Most of her girl friends are always out and about in the early afternoons, delivering their kids to various after-school activities, or knocking off a few errands before husbands are set free from jobs. As she wonders where everyone is today, Sara realizes that she's lost touch with many of her friends over the past weeks while caught up with the situation at home, the disruption in the family caused by Mark's condition. She pulls over in a Blockbuster parking lot, also strangely deserted for the time of day, and dials up the numbers of friends, moving through the digital address book in her cell phone one by one. No one answers.

Then it hits her, the fact that her friends have all found jobs. They've done the same thing she's doing today because their husbands all have the same disease Mark does. That much she knows for sure. About a month ago they'd held an emergency meeting over a catered lunch to address the situation and brainstorm possible solutions. All of them had heard about AMLS on the news, and were convinced their husbands had contracted the horrible disease. Sara remembers how, by the end of the meeting, most of her friends had decided to go out and get jobs, at least until a cure could be discovered by the government scientists. Parked in the video store parking lot, Sara wonders why she didn't feel driven to seek employment back then. For some reason she thought Mark would never fully succumb to the illness, that he would rise above it with the solid strength that had come to define him in her eyes, a definition now fading rapidly. It's time to feel desperate. AMLS is clearly defeating her husband. Her phone rings. One of her best friends, Laura Johnson, is calling back.

"Hi Laura," Sara answers.

"Sara – did you call?"

"I did – where are you?"

"At work," Laura states. "I got a job at City Hall . . .my husband hasn't got the disease yet, for some reason, but I got this job just in case – it doesn't seem like any man is safe these days . . ."

"No, it doesn't," Sara agrees, noticing the shiver in her spine. A man that might have a shot at resisting the illness would be Mick Johnson, the most masculine man Sara has ever met.

"How's it going?"

"Oh Sara, I just love it. It's mostly women in the offices here now . . .and we're having a blast – you should come by and fill out an application – a few more positions have opened this week. The men can't seem to show up for work anymore!"

"What's your title?"

"Right now I'm just a clerk – but I might run for mayor next year . . ."

Sara shakes her head. Her friend, little blond Laura Johnson, wants to be the mayor of their town. The idea of power rushes into Sara from out of nowhere. Not one to seek out the high in a burst of feeling, she can't help but give in to the urges beginning to rage inside her, the fierce desire to become a provider, like the female lions she'd learned about on The Discovery Channel.

"I'll be right over," she announces to her friend as she pulls out of the Blockbuster parking lot.

The same afternoon Mark, convinced Sara threatens the safe world of his backyard, loads his boys into the car with the promise of a camping trip. They head northwest towards British Columbia, to the country Mark heard about recently on the nightly news, a regular topic of coverage ever since Rupert Jones' breakthrough interview with Hillary Clinton.

Going against the passionate advice of both his wife and his aides, the president decides to stay at his Midwest ranch indefinitely. There he grudgingly agrees to their request that he undergo a medical evaluation. When the White House doctor tests his testosterone levels, the results show his production has halted entirely. Beth-Ann sinks into worry. Her husband has two years remaining in his second term and is in no position to lead a country. She begins taking long walks through the cornfields thinking about Hillary Clinton, her secret idol. What would the strong, brilliant woman do in such a situation? Stuck at the ranch with her incapacitated husband, her children missing weeks of school, Beth-Ann ponders striking out to track Hillary down in order to ask for advice and counsel on the situation.

Her husband hasn't told her the location of New America, even though he knows exactly where the country is situated. His spies told his aides and his aides told him, over and over, urging him to take some kind of action against the renegade nation. But during her periods of intense domestic isolation since moving into the White House five years before, Beth-Ann has come to form tight relationships with many of her husband's closest advisors. She will simply ask one of them where New America is located. Then she'll hitchhike there if she has to. The way her husband's been acting over the past weeks, Beth-Ann wonders if he might not even object to her taking such a trip. In fact, his only request ends up being that she leave the kids home at the ranch with him. He can't stand being apart from his children ever since contracting the disease that's changing the world.

Raised in a conservative, South Carolina family, Beth-Ann has never done anything as risky and adventurous as hitchhiking. The closest was when she spent a summer month traveling Europe with her best girlfriend. Walking out the half-mile driveway of the presidential ranch she feels the jitters rising up through her middle. She walks faster, because moving makes the jitters go down. When she reaches the end of the driveway and stands under the marble entranceway to the ranch she drops her pack to the ground, the frame pack she hasn't worn since the Europe trip. She sits down on the cushioned backpack. A few rattling pickup trucks drive by, slowing to see if her thumb is out before moving along, but Beth-Ann has her nervous thumbs tucked into her palms. Her fear and hesitation stem not from being a woman about to put herself into an incredibly vulnerable position with random men, but from her distinct need for comfort in a vehicle. She's never ridden in anything worth less than fifty grand. She's used to chauffeured Town Cars, Mercedes limousines, and private jets. She can't ride in a pickup truck. Afraid of dust and grease, the smell of gasoline makes her seasick with nausea. So she keeps her thumbs hidden for the next five hours while lonely, curious farmers slow to stare her down. She studies the horizon religiously until she spots a Cadillac with Texas plates seemingly emerging from the sunset. The white '65 Coupe Deville pulls over. Beth-Ann shoulders her backpack and steps to the driver's side window. An elderly couple smiles up at her.

"She told me to pull over," the man driving says, slowly removing his wrinkled hand from his wife's kneecap. "Didn't know we'd be stoppin' for the first lady of the United States, though."

"But I told you it was her," his wife whispers into his shoulder.

"Where are you folks heading?" Beth-Ann asks as politely as she can, eyeing the plush leather and polished wood interior, breathing in the air-conditioned coolness. She wonders if maybe this smiling couple can just take her all the way to British Colombia.

"Mount Rushmore," announces the man behind the wheel. "Ever seen it?"

Beth-Ann shakes her head.

"Maybe they'll carve your husband in up there someday, dear," the woman says. "There's room for another president, and he certainly deserves it more than any other man that's led this nation in a very long time."

"Oh, why, thank you," Beth-Ann says.

"Get on in then," the old man says, nodding at the back seat. Beth-Ann opens the door, slides her pack across the seat, and climbs into the delicious leather comfort of the Cadillac.

After driving through the night with them, Beth-Ann convinces the protesting couple to drop her off at the Marriot in Bismarck. They can't believe that she doesn't want to see the national landmark they've driven over a thousand miles to see.

"Maybe after my husband's carved in up there," is her earnest excuse.

After a lengthy picture session with the Texans, Beth-Ann settles into her comfy room for the night. She's up at dawn the next day, and takes a cab to a Highway 40 on-ramp, where she expects to spend all day waiting for an acceptable vehicle to ride further west in. But before noon she flips a confident thumb at a shiny black Lexus. Mark Reynolds slows to a stop in the breakdown lane. His boys lean forward to ask him what's going on.

"Looks like a lady needs a ride," Mark says calmly, lowering his window as Beth-Ann leans down closer.

"Nice car," she says.

"Oh, thanks – you can have it if you want – once we make it to New America."

His kids cheer raucously when they hear the name of their destination. Beth-Ann lifts her eyebrows and smiles, noticing the same disregard for material possessions in this stranger that she'd been seeing in her husband's recent behavior.

"That's exactly where I'm heading," she announces.

"Come with us, then," Mark says, slapping the seat beside him. When she gets in the car he turns to face her, his altered mind straining with a blur of recognition.

"Why do you look so familiar?" he asks her. She giggles, thinking it's a joke.

By the end of their two-day drive into B.C., Beth-Ann and the Reynolds family have formed a tight bond. For the boys, who feel like they've lost a mother in exchange for gaining a father, the cheery, traditional woman with a southern accent becomes a temporary replacement for Sara. And Beth-Ann enjoys the mothering tendencies that Mark's boys bring out in her, making it easier to be away from her own children. At some point during the drive, after Mark has realized who she is, it becomes clear to Beth-Ann why his name sounds so familiar.

"My husband wanted to hire you to be his attorney in a lawsuit he was considering filing, what would have been the first suit ever filed by a president while in office – he was told that you were the best," she says. Her forehead presses into the glass. Fields of wheat stream past. Mark blushes, then becomes serious.

"What would the case have been?" he asks her.

"The United States versus Dr. Yomi Nguyen, a chemist."

"He dropped it?"

Beth-Ann nods.

"Why?" Mark prods. She turns to face him. Her eyes are wet with tears.

"He contracted AMLS - thanks to her, of course," she says, looking down at her feet. "Now he doesn't want to do anything besides cook and play with our kids and take nature walks."

Mark stares straight ahead, expressionless. His boys are no longer giggling in the back seat.

"Isn't that what you have, daddy?" the youngest blurts out.

Mark clenches the steering wheel tight. They drive on in silence.

The president receives an unannounced guest during his sabbatical at the ranch. He comes downstairs one morning to find the Saudi sheikh sitting in his favorite chair. He shivers when they shake hands. Like usual the Arab's slick style, his linen suit, designer sunglasses, and deep tan, intimidates the president for an initial moment. The Sheik returns to a seated position.

"Can I get you anything?" the president asks, his voice weak. He remembers how he always kept the sheikh's favorite beverage, chai tea, at the White House for their secret meetings. There isn't any chai tea at the ranch.

"No, I am fine," Ali Munabib says. The president sits nervously on the couch. He doesn't trust this man, his father's old friend with eyes that remind him of a cobra.

"So, what can I do for you, Ali?"

"I am here on behalf of my country, Saudi Arabia – we are wondering about your plan in response to the gas crisis going on here in America."

"Well, the Alliance wants me to invade Venezuela next, while continuing to buy oil from your country, of course."

"And how do you feel about that?"

"I feel . . ."

The president gazes out the back windows at the flowing grasses of his backyard and the fields of crops beyond. He doesn't want to start another war. He just wants to be outside.

"I feel that it's time for something new – out here, I've been thinking about the sun and the wind, actually – they can power things."

The sheikh rises abruptly, his body tense with fury.

"Don't be stupid, Mr. President. Your country will die without oil. The United States will be bankrupt without my country's money, and your friends will abandon you. You must do what we request – there is one more neighbor of ours that has to be neutralized with force. I think you know what country I'm talking about – if we don't see you moving forward with the next war you promised us, a war your father pledged a decade ago, then our oil and our money will be taken away. And, in case your aides have failed to tell you, the consequences for your economy will be drastic – so please, don't be stupid."

The sheikh walks out of the living room, exiting as silently and mysteriously as he'd entered. The president, paralyzed by fear and confusion, cradles his face in his palms. All he can think about is walking barefoot through the prairie grasses, stalking butterflies.

A few days later he receives a call from George Sanders, CEO of Exxon and board member of the Alliance.

"How's my home state?" the president asks.

"Eh, things are changing here too, old pal – but the porterhouses and pistols and oil pumps ain't going anywhere, as long as things keep heading our way."

The president has lost his longing for the steaks and guns and oil fields of Texas. He feels more at home on his ranch in Kansas, a location that had originally been his wife's idea, a place to escape where no one would know them.

"What can I do for you, Colonel?" he asks, employing Sanders' nickname.

"I don't want to bother you, Mr. President, sir, only to inform you of the Alliance's two-pronged plan to double our financial resources – first, we will be making a military move to claim the Polar Ice Cap as a private source of freshwater for the American people – in the process we hope to neutralize this New America we've all been hearing too much about."

"But they have no real army," the president counters. He followed Rupert's week-long report almost as closely as his wife.

"I think you're getting soft out there on the prairie. We don't care about their lack of defenses - they're a threat on a different level," the Colonel fires back. "Our second goal is to bolster the storm-making technology our scientists have already been successful with in the Gulf of Mexico – if we can continue bombarding the Southern coast with bigger hurricanes, it will be the perfect excuse to double gas prices – we have to clean up over the next decade, before those hydrogen cell bastards take over."

"I'm not sure I approve of either plan," the president says, his voice lacking any kind of true authority.

"Well, pardner, your vote in the Alliance only counts as one – and, unlike your other job, there is no such thing as a veto."

"Do what you want," the president says, tired. He hangs the phone up gently. Anger has no place to gain a foothold within his body's altered chemistry. But something about his back-to-back interactions with these two men has left a very sour taste in his mouth. He goes outside to chew on some grass.

Trying to rest at his apartment in D.C. for a few days, taking a break from the rigorous schedule he's maintained for months, Rupert is bombarded by calls from people back home in Louisiana. These aren't contacts from the vacuum sale days, but old friends and acquaintances from his youth, good people within his mother's concentric social circles. When Rupert is dropped off at the end of his mama's muddy driveway after hitching a ride from the New Orleans bus station, he's first greeted by a howling bunch of hound dogs baying from the rickety front porch. His mother steps out and quiets them. Mrs. Jones is a round ball of a woman clothed in a flower print dress. A red checkered apron is tied around her waist. Her long, tight braids of hair descend down beyond her bulbous behind. Silencing the dogs with a few sharp shushes, she ambles to the top of the decaying stairs and spreads her gyrating arms. She stands there waiting, grinning. Rupert drops his duffel bag in the mud, climbs the stairs, and lets himself fall into her embrace. After squeezing him tight she steps back and holds him by the shoulders.

"Rupert Mason Jones – damn fine to see you, boy!"

"Are you surprised?"

"Not a bit. Thought you might be comin' around to check on your old ma after another bout a' dem rains . . ."

She nods past him at the soaked landscape surrounding the little shack. The branches sag with soggy leaves. Water oozes from the ground.

"You've stayed here the whole time? Through all these storms?"

"Oh yeah – someone's gotta hold down this fort asides these yappin' mutts, right?"

"Sure, ma. I'm proud of you. I'm here to see you – but there's another reason I came back home – to look into something our friends down here have been sharing with me."

Rupert backs down the steps to retrieve his duffel bag as the dogs romp and play in the front yard.

"And what might that be?" his mother asks.

Rupert climbs back up the stairs to whisper his next words into his mother's ear.

"It looks like our government made that Carolina storm, mama. And the others before it . . .they're making more as we speak."

"And how'd they go about playing God like that, son?"

"I'm not sure – but it's what I'm here to find out – let's go inside and I'll tell you all about it."

Rupert's mother, a roly-poly jumble of excess flesh, is all joy over having her son back home. Her red plaid apron and flour-stained hands and wide beaming smile are the foundation of her nature. She raised eleven boys in her day, all of whom have since flown the coop. So her motherly urges, pent up for the past few years, gush out in response to her first-born's arrival. She slathers Rupert with love, and like every good mother this love is mostly in the form of food. During his first twenty-four hours in her house she makes him buttermilk biscuits and black bean soup, fried chicken and mashed potatoes, catfish, hominy grits, and braised greens. Rupert finds himself forced to eat something new practically every hour. Having long ago shed the dietary habits of his youth in the deep south in exchange for a more sophisticated diet of sushi and salads, Rupert is surprised that his stomach can even handle this overload. But the most prevalent ingredient in everything his mother feeds him is love, making the digestion of all these thousands of calories an effortless task. But after little more than a full day of receiving this overzealous pampering, Rupert begins rising before dawn to spend long days investigating this secret, storm-making technology of the U.S. government.

He hooks up with a scrappy shipbuilder known only as Smitty, who curbs his creole to speak in understandable English, albeit with a thick Cajun accent. Smitty expertly guides Rupert through the array of docks and warehouses fanning out from the flooded City of

Saints. Hiding behind giant crates and inside the skeletal hulls of unfinished tankers, on their fifth day together Rupert and his guide stumble upon the two hovering aircraft being worked on in the middle of a boat-building warehouse turned hangar. But instead of the classic spying planes both men have seen in photographs, these planes have noticeable differences. The radar disk is underneath the belly rather than on top of the wings, and is sharply curved into a half-moon shape. Hiding in a maintenance closet among brooms and cleaning fluids, Rupert cracks the door and snaps off a full roll of pictures.

"I've gotta' ask someone about these planes – I mean, these pictures really don't prove anything . . ."

"Geez we've got to be careful on dis one – I'm risking my job to be here. My company thinks I'm on vacation in Disney World – just wanted to sit at the crick cathin' catfish for a week, and now you're interruptin' me!"

"But you don't work for this dock, Smitty . . ."

"No matter – all these companies are in cahoots, sharing unions and that kinda' thing."

"Well, get back there in the shadows and hide – I'm gonna go ask that guy cleaning the wing a few questions."

"For shit sake," the Cajun grumbles, crouching down in a pile of used mop heads as Rupert closes the door behind him. He approaches the balding, paunchy man high up on a ladder scrubbing the wing of a strange aircraft.

"Hey, you mind if I interrupt you for a second, my friend?" Rupert shouts up to him.

"Sure thing. Anything to distract me from scrubbing all this goddamn titanium steel."

The man with a pot belly and an unrecognizable accent, not Jersey or California but something in between, climbs down the ladder slowly. When he reaches the floor he offers Rupert a firm handshake.

"Charley Summers."

"Charely – Rupert Jones. Pleasure."

"So, what do ya want to know?"

"You're not gonna ask me why I want to know it?"

"Eh, that's your own business, really – just as long as I keep my job. All the big shots are off today. It's a down day. But to be honest with you, all I know is what these babies can do. Not why they can do it."

"That's okay. I've got a good idea why. I just need you to tell me what."

"It's simple, really," Charley says, pulling out a Malrboro from a crushed pack. He offers one to Rupert, who politely declines. After he sparks the smoke both men look up.

"The giant discs under the belly here, well, you'll be interested to know that instead of producing sonar waves to spy on enemy communication, they produce gravity – they're miniature versions of the fucking moon! Real powerful waves of gravity come off these babies. Trust me, I helped test 'em. They fly 'em out over the Gulf and . . .well, the rest is a mystery to me."

Charley shifts into a whisper.

"So, now that I told you what, you tell me why . . .They messin' with the tides out there or something?"

Rupert shakes his head.

"They're messing with the weather."

Beth-Ann arrives in New America just as the country's constitution is in the process of being drafted. She is welcomed to the initial meeting of the Inner Circle, the group of women that will form the core of the government. Beth-Ann is invited as an honorary guest in the underground conference chambers. Insecure at the start, she eventually settles in amongst all the confident women seated like fashion-conscious knights at a high-tech round table, in awe over her close proximity to her secret idol Hillary Clinton. The main topic of concern is sustainability, a concept the Inner Circle has declared to be of the utmost priority in organizing the culture and society of their newborn country. The meeting occurs in a space designed to emulate a womb, an oval carved into the rocky soil and lit by solar-powered bulbs. There the women unite around their focused efforts to clearly see the steps necessary to create a document of such intense importance, one that will define the future course of their newborn nation. Once they unite their collective intuitions the rest flows easily.

The outcome of the week-long meeting is a guide for governing, what the women call a Blueprint For All Tomorrows, where the priority is placed on the children before anything else. Measures are taken to ensure the education, health, and nurtured freedom of every child in the country. The second focus is the natural environment. This founding document declares nature must always be considered before any interests of the country or its citizens. The third major item of importance, tackled on the final day, is the establishment of an economy based not on capitalism or, for that matter, on any economic structure previously employed by a society. What they develop is a system based on a reward-for-experience philosophy, where money and time are doled out to the citizens on a scale based upon proposed activities and the intent to fully experience them. The entire economy is to be focused on the stockpiling of capital for funding an endless stream of grants and fellowships. Every citizen has the chance, instead of working, to make proposals to pursue various worthy adventures. The only requirement is that these approved experiences are documented in some fashion, and then shared with the community upon completion.

Of course, some people have to do the work required to keep the country moving forward as a functioning society. The original fifty citizens occupy the top-most level of New American society. They don't have to engage in any kind of work, and are free to apply for the experience grants. The entry-level citizens, on the other hand, must work in a chosen area, something he or she feels competent in and enjoys doing. These initiates work to sustain the community, their only pay being membership to the nation, a qualification that ensures essential needs, such as health care and education, are met. After a period of time, given that reliability and performance standards are achieved, these newcomers move up into a position where they are able to begin applying for the experience grants, and the next round of immigrants takes over the practical tasks involved with running the country. The women cover all these bases over the course of the week as they build the foundation of a potential Utopia. Beth-Ann catches as many pieces of the meeting as she can, although being so close to Hillary is extremely distracting. She wonders if anyone else is noticing the glow, the halo that seems to constantly surround Mrs. Clinton. Beth-Ann has to avert both her eyes and her mind, at the same time enjoying the exhilaration of what feels like an elementary school crush. Her heart sinks when Hillary leaves the group repeatedly to deal with her administrative affairs, sometimes not returning until the next day. Beth-Ann searches desperately for sleep in an effort to make the night go by faster, eager for morning, for the gift of another day spent in the same room with her idol.

In Houston, the Colonel's home base, things are changing in the same way they are across metropolitan centers nationwide. A slow and steady takeover of the building is happening right below him. His office used to be on the second floor of the downtown high rise. Now he occupies the twenty-eighth, the highest floor in the building. The other twenty-seven are staffed entirely by the women that now dominate most levels of the company. They are the majority in every department. Sanders is still the CEO, a king holding his ground in a dying monarchy, but he doesn't saunter through the building like he used to, hands on his hips, overseeing employees that doubled as his scotch and cigar buddies. If he did happen to roam past the various divisions of Exxon's headquarters today, The Colonel would notice the subtle changes in color and texture. He would hear classical music seeping out of invisible speakers. He'd see walls and ceilings sponge-painted in muted colors, and coffee corners that have been converted into aromatic nooks stocked with tea and scones, where soft conversations last through whole afternoons. The women consciously place more importance on face-to- face discussions with one another than on returning e-mails and voice mail messages from other time zones. Homemade food fills the refrigerators and is warmed up at lunch hour on kitchenette stoves. The building hums with a collective feminine thrust as the women try to guide the company forward into the realm of sustainable energy.

The Colonel paces above them all, yakking on the phone with one of his cohorts in the Alliance about the performance of what he likes to call The Hurricane Maker.

"Let's make more of them," he bellows into his headset telephone.

"George, the storms have worked to our advantage up to this point, aside from all the fatalities, I guess you could say – but, honestly, now the ports are seriously damaged all along the coast

– if we unleash more storms we won't even be making a profit at four dollars a gallon – we can't go to four dollars a gallon."

"Fuck!"

Sanders is smart enough to know that Ralph Wiley, chief engineer of the Alliance's weather-producing technology, is a man to be taken seriously.

"And, besides, we're changing weather patterns across North America – half of Canada is currently experiencing a severe drought, in fact . . ."

"Which half?" the Colonel asks, perking up.

"The western, sir."

"Perfect. Keep making the storms until further notice."

"Yes, sir."

From the Colonel's skewed perspective, watching New America die along with his beloved oil would even some kind of score in a game he has no clue how to win.

Out over the Gulf two planes hover low over the ocean, a few hundred yards apart. Concealed by midnight darkness, there are no lights flashing on the wings, nothing to give away their secret purpose. The pilots are aware of everything around them thanks to night vision technology and advanced radar. At a coordinated point in time they engage the gravity-making discs. A slow rumbling builds under their feet as the disks angle towards the open ocean between the two planes. Screens display images from night vision cameras. The pilots watch waves swell up in reaction to this manmade gravity. The water rolls and boils in a great stew beneath them. On a separate set of monitors showing atmospheric conditions they watch moisture collect in the space between them, an enormous, water-soaked cloud growing, swelling, becoming an entity of swirling winds, lightning and thunder. The planes are losing their hold on the beast of a cloud as it grows into a full-blown storm ready to be set free. The Alliance's meteorological consultants chose this night based on jet stream patterns and the desired landing point for this particular storm. The computers in the planes tell the pilots exactly when the storm is ready to be released, when it has reached a point of enough stability to maintain itself without the planes that produced it.

"Ready to initiate the countdown?"

"Roger, Roger – "

"What's your vector, Victor?"

The pilots chuckle after their usual reference to Airplane, The Movie.

"T-minus sixty seconds – ready to initiate when you are . . ."

"Initiate away!"

Sixty seconds later the lunar discs shift back to a neutral position. Gravity production ceases, and the planes bank away in opposite directions. The storm, now free, pulls moisture into itself, water droplets that otherwise would have drifted on their own natural course to become rain showers over the heartland of the Northern Hemisphere. Instead the jet stream guides the hurricane steadily towards the Gulf Coast of Florida and the city of Tampa Bay.

Maria's act of giving birth, from conception to the moments after her son is born, moments that quickly transform themselves into days and weeks of happiness, easily becomes the most profound experience of her life. It excites her more than any conversation she's ever had with God. In fact, since returning from Colombia pregnant with her first child, she's stopped hearing God's voice in their house or in the rafters of her church. Having quit her job as a priest, she now only visits the church once a week for the Sunday morning service. She doesn't mind that her intense connection with divinity seems to be over, at least for the time being. There will be plenty of opportunity for one-on-one discussions later in life, when she'll listen once again for the voice she could never forget no matter how long she lives, an angel's song blended with the wind, feminine and masculine woven into one.

Now Maria has something more important to do than listen to God. Her newborn child, and the next one already forming in her fertile womb, have altered her chemistry, making it necessary to live deaf to heaven's sirens. She's become entirely focused on what lives and breathes around her, on her husband, his dog, her cats, their baby. Her ears press to the ground instead of cocking towards the sky. She knows that to lift them back up and fix her radar on the calls of heaven once again would take long stretches of solitude, an extremity of discipline and, worst of all, moods as volatile as the Vermont weather. Maria can't subject her growing family to that. So she lets go of the spirit world, what has been her life's most primary focus, and her ears open up to a new voice, one that speaks from the center of her heart.

With one child born and another already on the way, as they concentrate their energies on the new life growing within the log walls of their home, Ben wonders why it doesn't feel like he and his wife are at the place they've always wanted to be. All the pieces are seemingly weaving together, but for Ben, something lurks beneath. He yearns to be somewhere else. His books don't satisfy him anymore. His view is changing. It likely has been for some time, and his new perspective, induced by his days with the *mamas*, is making him see the subtle alterations in the scene below. Spring has sprung but many trees remain leafless, lifeless, victims of the acid rain drifting in from the Midwest. New colors accent the horizon, strange shades of orange and red, carbon monoxides trapped by the atmosphere, lingering on the horizon to confine the extent of his view. But the most dramatic change in his vista, by far, is a new road being cut through the landscape below. Ben had heard about the possibility of its construction, but never thought it would actually take place. This is Vermont. New roads don't happen, especially paved ones. But a road now slices through his view, changing the color scheme by adding black asphalt to the mix of greens and browns. The worst part is he doesn't crave being inside their log cabin at the end of a day. Without the outlet of her career Maria has taken over some of his roles. Spending her days in the house with their son she's been preparing their evening meals ahead of time, so dinner waits for Ben when he steps in the door all covered in sawdust and mud. He doesn't know what to do with himself without the tasks of cooking and making a fire to consume the rest of his day's energy. He retreats to his books beside the woodstove fire that burns strong without his attending to it. But the only book he winds up reading every night is the Lonely Planet Guide to Colombia.

That spring Ben reinstates a ritual from their early years of dating. After dinner the couple gathers around their old radio in the living room to listen to Fresh Air on NPR. It isn't long before they hear the radio broadcast of Rupert Jones' second report on New America, the in-depth story aired nightly for an entire week that dispels some of the mystery about a country that has been little more than a rumor for almost a year. Ben and Maria miss hardly a single word of Rupert's week-long report on the new country. By the end of his stay Rupert decides to accept the Inner Circle's invitation to become the nation's first new citizen in over six months.

"Without knowing it, I've been waiting my entire life for this opportunity," he says at the conclusion of his report, adding, quite sentimentally, "Goodbye, America the Beautiful." Ben and Maria, having not missed a single word of the report, put their land on the market the next day.

The process of leaving their home in Vermont is harder than Ben had ever imagined. Forcing himself to rip up the roots he'd been plunging into the rocky soil for six years is the worst feeling he's ever experienced. He wants to bring everything with them – the network of trails he cut by hand, his forest and fields, his well, his view. He wants to lift up his cabin, root cellar and all, and take it with them. The walls he knows down to every nail, the floors he sanded, the woodstove he installed, the interlocking oak trunks making up the foundation that he felled with his chainsaw. But all he can take are his books and his dog. Ben would die without his books, and still they can't even fit half of his lifelong collection in the old Volkswagon bus they'll drive to British Columbia. Not able to part with any of the worn paperbacks, some with duck-taped spines, others with missing covers, he has them shipped ahead of time to New America. The night before leaving, the cabin stripped bare and a last fire consuming itself in the woodstove, Ben has Maria pick up a bottle of gin on her way home from her last day at the church. They eat take-out pizza on the floor, while Ben gets drunk for the first time in years, some part of his mind hoping the juniper berry spirit might be able to recreate the clarity that chewing coca produced in him. Instead he winds up outside on his back, watching the stars spin, ignoring his wife's requests that he come to bed, belting out old John Denver songs at the top of his lungs.

During the course of their drive westward in the coughing old van, a vehicle barely capable of highway speeds, Ben is numb with withdrawal. He lets Maria drive most of the way. He curls up in the back seat with his dog Al, re-reading Steinbeck books one after another, looking for peace of mind in the words of his all-time favorite writer.

Working their way around the world, Yomi and Eric live off the spirit of uncertainty and feed on the thrill of adventure. Shuttled around in private jets and high-speed yachts, watched out for by local dignitaries loyal to New America, their pace is swift and efficient. Moving west to east, they dose eastern European Mafia, the installed rulers of North Africa, and the princes of the Middle East. They are careful to leave alone tribal elders and warriors, native hunters and nomadic gypsies. Hard-working farmers are spared as well. In the cities, artists and thinkers are alerted to avoid the tap water through warnings whispered in dark Bohemian corners. Yomi is aware of testosterone's inherent relationship to creative energy and inspiration, and a world without art strikes her as a concept even worse than a world ruled by men. So any men the couple decides to be living inspired, purposeful lives are saved during this nine month whirlwind, an approach that works just fine until they reach China.

The overwhelming population of the recently industrialized country, combined with the sprawling landscape, proves daunting to both of them. Sweating in a dirty Shanghai hotel room, Yomi paces while Eric spreads the maps of local watersheds out on the king size bed. The faded maps are covered with criss-crossing rivers like the veins on the back of an old person's hand. Chinese characters run along the top and bottom. Their translator and guide, set up for them in every region by New American contacts, failed to show up at their rendezvous spot the day before. Overwhelmed by frustration, Eric slams a fist into one of the maps.

"There's close to a billion men right here in this country, but I have no idea how we're going to get them . . ."

Yomi stops pacing. She's been waiting for this moment.

"I know how," she says, a peculiar glint in her eye.

"Please – enlighten me."

She bends down to unzip a leather doctor's bag she's been carrying with them ever since they left New America to resume their mission. She pulls out a glass tube. Eric lifts his eyebrows.

"What'cha' got there, girl?"

"Remember all those hours I spent in the lab before we left?"

"I couldn't forget them if I tried."

"I turned the drug into a gas," she says, lifting the tube. "This amount right here should be enough to take care of the northern half of Asia - we just have to forget about saving the usual handfuls – they all get it."

"So where will I go to breathe?"

"With me – to the Himalayas! The gas won't make it up there. I designed it to be neutralized above ten thousand feet. The only men living up there are celibate monks anyway."

"All right, what the hell," Eric says, shrugging his shoulders, crumpling up the watershed maps into a ball and tossing them out the window. A week later, when Yomi decides the weather patterns are right, they crack a tube on the sidewalk, slip on gas masks, and jump on a high speed train that will whisk them to the border with Nepal. There they will make their way up to a monastery she knows of on the side of Anapurna, where they'll wait out the month-long diffusion of Yomi's vaporous drug across the northern half of Asia's atmosphere.

In the Himalayas Yomi loses her focus entirely, confusing up with down, left with right, death with life. The world of Buddhist prayer flags blowing in breezes carried on the backs of deities millennia old, a place where white jaguars slip across snow fields and monks chant by candlelight, has a strongly seductive power. Rupert Jones, still frustrated by NPR's refusal to break his recently completed, epic story on the Alliance's secret storm-making technology in the Gulf, takes off from British Columbia on his own assignment to track down the scientists. Eager to test the waters of global journalism, he uses his connections in New America to determine their exact coordinates on the side of Anapurna. Aware of the contaminated air, his informants advise him to wear a breathing mask until he reaches ten thousand feet. So Rupert, in his gas mask, follows two sherpas he hired in Kathmandu up twisting mule paths for three days. Upon reaching the monastery he's in better shape than ever before in his life. He takes his time befriending the scientists, joining them for meals and meditations, gradually gaining their dual trust inside the alternate reality of the monastery, the frankensence-scented, ethereal world of bells and chants and candles. At night they huddle together outside to watch the stars explode in the sky.

While Eric and Rupert engage in the meditations and songs, eating the vegetarian food in silent sessions, they mostly go through the motions of it all, observing Yomi's burgeoning infatuation with the Buddhist state of mind. She's becoming more enthralled with the rhythms of monastic life by the day. Eric takes note of the changes with a degree of trepidation. Her eyes begin to glaze over with a translucent layer of passivity. Her pupils widen. Her stomach shrinks as she subsists on the bare minimum diet, nothing besides brown rice and steamed greens and water. Her feet seem to barely strike the stone floors so that her walking is closer to floating. But when a month has passed, ensuring a safe return for them down to civilization, Yomi shows no signs of being ready to leave. When Eric confronts her about this growing state of detachment one night in their room, she silences him with her hand.

"It's a phase, Eric, one I need to pursue for a little time. Rupert will document it all. You'll be able to hear all about it in his report – or maybe it will be a book."

"Fuck the book, Yomi – we have a job to finish, and you're flaking out on it!" Eric shouts.

"I'm not flaking out, Eric – I just need a break, that's all – "

"Yeah, a break to get high on Ohms and satisfy your ego!"

"Stop yelling!" Yomi hisses. "It's against the rules to raise your voice."

Eric flops back on the stiff-as-a-board bed.

"That's right – celibate monks don't have anything to raise their voices about – frickin' weirdos."

"Shut up."

Tensions between the two of them build exponentially by the day. Once a week has passed, beginning to feel like their friend, Rupert addresses his wish to be the one who tells their story.

"As you can see, I didn't bring any cameras or crew or any of that stuff up here . . . you guys need to finish what you're doing without the distraction of a nosy reporter like me."

Sitting on the monastery roof, playing hooky to that morning's dawn chant in the gathering room beneath them, the chorus of ohms pulsating through the roof they're sitting on, Eric gazes up at the jagged snow and rock summit of Anapurna, Everest looming beyond. Yomi listens intently to the reporter. She feels his eyes taking her in, aware that this man holds the attention of the entire world with every new story he reports, aware that her story is the one the world wants to know most.

"But after we're done you can record my . . . our story, right?" she asks.

"Right. Someone has to share your story with the world, just like someone had to write the Bible. I want to be that person."

"Are you comparing me to Jesus?" Yomi asks, her voice detaching from some grounded level of reality. Eric snaps his head to face her.

"Yomi, we should probably address this after we're done, after we get back home."

Yomi continues to face Rupert, focusing her energy in his direction.

"It has to be just how I want it to be! I'll be the star, I hope."

"Of course."

Eric shivers. He hates this new distance underlying his wife's voice. This is the woman in whose basket he's placed all of his eggs. He takes a deep breath, trying to center himself.

"Don't worry, you'll be the co-star, Eric," Rupert says carefully, trying to maintain a pleasant atmosphere between the three of them.

"We really should start right now!" Yomi states. "What do you want to know first? Where I got the inspiration to do this? I'll tell you . . ."

"Yomi!" Eric says firmly, standing up. His wife doesn't acknowledge him, consumed by the false rush of fame. Rupert shifts uncomfortably, unable to wriggle out of the hole he's accidentally plunged himself into.

"A river gave me the idea," she blurts out. "I never would have believed water could speak. But it can. My husband knows all about that – maybe he can chime in on this part."

"Don't drag me into this, Yomi," Eric snaps, furious that she's never shared this detail of her life with him, something so directly related to their intimate connection. "We're not even finished with what we started . . ."

"It's time for a break," she says, smiling haphazardly at both men.

"You're cra – "

"Go ahead, say it – call me crazy – but make sure you give Rupert here the real story about who the crazy one is in this relationship."

Eric storms over to the edge of the roof before she's finished her words. Poised above the rope ladder leading down to the interior courtyard below, he addresses her one last time.

"I'm leaving – are you coming or staying?"

"I think I'll stay," Yomi answers without hesitation.

"Fine."

Eric disappears over the edge.

"Eric!" Rupert shouts, standing up. "What are yo – "

"Let him go," Yomi says, reaching out to pull the reporter back down to a seated position. "Where were we? Did you say you brought a tape recorder?"

Rupert shakes his head.

Trying to ignore the pain of abandonment and rejection, Eric leaves Yomi there at the monastery. In disbelief that she's let him go so easily, he heads out on a journey to explore his own desire for extremity. Wandering south, Eric lingers in Buddhist temples and on tropical beaches, indulging his senses while taking care to avoid the many smiling temptresses he comes across, steering clear of inviting brothels, trying hard to stay true to his wife perched on the side of a Himalayan peak. Eventually he winds up in Bali. In Singaraja, a small, coastal village yet to be invaded by pleasure seeking foreigners, Eric settles down. He befriends the local fishermen, and joins them at sea in an attempt to confront and conquer his intense fear of the ocean. He spends his nights with these same men in the town's only bar, a thatch-roofed bungalow behind the beach. In this tiki-torch-lit, open-air tavern, during a late night talk over the local beer, Eric sees Kaliana dancing alone in a dark corner. The fishermen speak of her in hushed words of reverence. They purposefully avert their eyes as long as she's in the room. By the time Eric rises to approach her she's vanished into the night, her brown skin blending into the blackness, her sequined dress a mirage of tiny fading mirrors.

As Eric listens closely to the fishermen's descriptions of this mystical creature over the weeks to follow, a woman who once supposedly dwelled in a coral cave on the ocean floor, he can't help but be intrigued. The seriousness of how they speak about her convinces him that she truly is a sex priestess like they proclaim, a character straight out of *The Epic Of Gilgamesh.* But the rumors of her origin vary greatly. The most dramatic, far fetched tale of Kaliana's beginning describes her being conceived from a lonely sailor's teardrop ingested by a giant oyster and converted into a pearl, from which spawned the mermaid-like seductress. On the opposite end of the spectrum is the story that she's simply a wayward prostitute from Jakarta with a passion for the sea, and told all her panting customers over the years about the underwater cave she planned on constructing with their loose money. Eric prods the fishermen as he waits to spot her slinking about the bar again, her dark skin blending into the night, the silver sequined dress catching slivers of light, a beacon in the dark. The prevailing notion in the village is that Kaliana is ready to take on her first apprentice in almost five years. After questioning the fishermen more, Eric learns the only two requirements of any potential student: he must be a foreigner, and he has to know how to scuba dive. The day after making this discovery Eric takes a bus to a resort town up the coast, where he books a three-day scuba diving course. Although already an expert diver before taking the class, he has an intense fear about diving in the ocean, and needs to be guided into it gently. On the second and third days of instruction, the class makes underwater excursions that Eric joins for as long as required before surfacing anxiously. After receiving his certificate of completion he heads back into town.

One lonely night in the town bar a few days later, while his fishermen friends are occupied in a secret shack playing a local card game involving heavy bets of the next day's catch, Eric is a few beers deep. His head hangs over the worn wood table as he pens a note to Yomi alerting her of his location in case she decides to find him. Eventually he's approached by an American with long hair and sun-bronzed skin.

"Mind if I have a seat?"

Eric grunts something close enough to a yes, not bothering to lift up his head. The hippie with a New England accent takes a seat.

"Eh, headin' up to teach English in Pattaya, got myself a full time job for once – those Thai girls had better watch out after where I've been – hey, what's got you down, man?"

"I saw this woman in here a few weeks back, but I haven't spotted her since. She moved like a cat, like the most exotic feline I've ever seen. My fishermen buddies call her Kaliana – heh, they've got all sorts of stories about . . ."

Eric notices the American's face brighten with recognition at the sound of her name.

"Oh man, you can stop right there, the stories are true – I almost became her apprentice – just came up a little short somehow – but it was still the best thirty days of my life, by far. She's the Kama Sutra brought alive, man, I can't even explain it, except to say that she kept me wanting to know more and more of her, even after weeks of indulging, having her beauty all to myself – I couldn't get enough. You should definitely check her out – she'll change your life. I can show you where to find her," the American adds with a knowing wink.

"But I've got a woman," Eric protests. "I'm a married man." As he says the words he sees Kaliana's curves imprinted on his long-term memory. The flashing glimpse of her in his mind's eye overrides a year's worth of Yomi memories.

"Are you happy?" the long hair Yankee asks, glancing down at the gold marriage band on Eric's finger.

"Yes – no – well, I was . . ."

"What happened, if you don't mind me asking?"

"She left me, in a way – not physically, really - she's hanging out with a reporter and a bunch of monks on the side of Anapurna."

"Wow. Well, all the better reason for you to pursue the tutelage of Kaliana – if she lets you go down to her cave, and I'm talking about the one on the ocean floor, not the one between her legs – you won't have any more problems once you see your wife again. In fact, I don't think any woman will be able to resist devoting themselves to you then. I wasn't lucky enough to reach that level of instruction. Heh, all I did was miss one night with her 'cause I got too drunk right here at this bar . . . "

Eric glances around, unsure how to react. He realizes that during the course of their conversation women have been looking his new friend up and down. Blond German tourists and local barmaids alike have been subtly studying the traveler's features. Some of the more daring ones are beginning to drift closer, moths drawn to the flame of his awakened sensuality. Something profound must have taken place during that month with Kaliana. Groveling at the depths of abandonment, more excited about getting drunk than he'd ever been during his darkest days as a PHD student, all Eric wants is whatever knowledge this wanderer has acquired.

The next evening Eric lets Kaliana's former apprentice lead him to her one-room bungalow tucked into a grove of palm trees behind one of the more isolated local beaches. He's nervous as hell as he slips in through the hanging beads that make up the front door. A dramatic canopy bed occupies the middle of the room. Lying propped up on one elbow atop the bed is the renowned seductress. She draws him close with her large brown eyes and beckoning smile. A blend of Japanese, Indian, and indigenous islander, she is entirely naked except for a string of pearls around her middle. Her perfectly proportioned body is toned with strength yet billows with feminine curves. Eric approaches the bed tentatively.

"I've been waiting for you," Kaliana whispers once he's close enough to hear. Her breath is salty and sweet. Eric sits on the bed. When she slithers herself around him he immediately passes out in her arms.

When Eric wakes up later that night she sends him away with instructions to visit her each evening there in her bungalow. So he returns every night for a month of lessons that are surprisingly tame. His clothes stay on as she reads to him, passages from *Lolita*, Bukowski monologues, the poetry of Byron and Keats, and myths starring Aphrodite. She has him paint her naked body with finger paints, and her figure on a canvas in acrylics. She instructs him to write an essay on the nature of her beauty during his days, which he reads to her in nightly installments. Over this month of tutelage there are little more than a few light kisses exchanged between them, during which time Eric remains in utter awe over her combination of sophisticated intelligence and primal sensuality. During the days he often heads out on the water with his fisherman buddies, when he finds himself drifting absently away into daydreams of Kaliana. The fishermen shake their heads, laughing among themselves, sharing jokes in their native language.

One slow, humid night, while Eric contemplates heading back to the Himalayas to retrieve his wife, Kaliana invites him to her underwater cave.

"I don't bring all of my students there," she admits in her serpentine voice.

"Does that mean I passed the first phase?"

"You did."

"Why?"

"You showed up, every day for a month, just like I asked you to. Showing up is all love really asks of a man – showing up, then working hard at the life he's showing up for. You've proven your ability at both. All that takes is persistence. Persistence, and a little faith. I can show you how much further you'll go once you decide to never stop persisting – if you want . . ."

"I do."

A shiver of apprehension passes through Eric as he agrees to travel further down this path of decadence. So many days are going by where he and Yomi aren't showing up for their relationship, what he'd thought they both had faith in. This is her choice, he reminds himself. Yomi is choosing to show up for her premature interview and the chanting sessions of monks instead of their marriage and the project that had originally joined them. To keep his conscience clear Eric tells himself that by lingering in Nepal, blinded by hubris, she's forcing him to find his own avenues of engagement in her absence. These avenues, more like streets of a red light district, might seem much less pure than Yomi's turn down her side alleyways of Buddhism and fame. But Eric stays focused on the mantra he's grown into since turning thirty – *nothing is holy, everything is sacred.* His nights with Kaliana are sacred by all definitions of the word.

When Eric rents scuba gear in the village for the underwater journey the eyes of the locals watch him closely. That night Kaliana rows them out into the middle of the bay under a full moon. Wearing only a glass mask over her eyes, with a waterproof flashlight in one hand she takes his hand in the other and they dive down together. They swim to where the moonlight can't reach, to a place so different it could be another planet as far as Eric is concerned. The doorway to her cave is a series of red fabric curtains illuminated by watertight lanterns, swaying gently in the current, leading deep into a wall of coral. Eric swims behind her through this tunnel of red and finds himself in a great white room. The walls are smooth and polished. Stalactites and stalagmites dangle from the ceiling, ice blue and perspiring in drops of pure fresh water filtered by limestone over centuries of time. Kaliana shows him how she collects these drops in seashell cups and uses the water for drinking. Her diet, and Eric's during the weeks in her cavern, consists of only raw ingredients. She catches tuna and shark with her bare hands, filets them with a machete, and feeds the meat to him with seductive precision following the rounds of what become more hedonistic instruction on her seaweed bed inside the cave. She has him feed her oysters and then to drink from between her legs. He suckles on this liquid, the fruit of the ocean digested by her passion and converted into a sweet and salty elixir she releases in writhing, orgasmic waves. It's the most intoxicating substance Eric has ever stumbled upon, with effects that are more enlightening than mushrooms, more energizing than pure cocaine. Her secretions offer the comfort of the finest wine, soothe like opium, inspire as ecstasy does. Eric becomes an addict, and can't get enough of Kaliana.

What he can't get enough of during his time in the cave are her timeless lessons. She keeps him at just the right emotional distance to prevent him from falling in love. She stops talking when he wants to know too much about her. Sometimes she makes him go days without touching her, letting him get to the point of forgetting what her skin feels like, what her kisses taste like, until he begins to crave these sensations with all his being. In this way she teaches Eric the truest love he will ever know, never permanent, always passionate, like fire and ice joined together. She awakens his innermost sensuality and challenges him to control it, until he wakes up one day realizing that love and sex have finally united in his mind. Both terms intertwine and become one. It's as if, like Odysseus, Eric is able to listen to the sirens' song while surviving to tell the tale, except this priceless knowledge will prove to be fleeting, an elusive clarity he'll live the rest of his life without ever regaining.

Yomi has been at the monastery for almost three months when she finally snaps out of her trance like state. Rupert, frustrated by her growing inability to communicate any worthwhile information, has long since retreated to New America. The catalyst of Yomi's sudden awakening is a simple, profane event that momentarily parts the sacred atmosphere inside the monastery. One morning she's following the measured steps of the monks in the walking meditation of early afternoon. Reveling in the placid waters of her quiet brain, she's startled when the monk pacing in front of her emits a loud fart. The quick squeeze of his butt cheeks is unable to stop its release, and the holy silence is broken. The group maintains composure, continuing forward with the meditation as if nothing has happened. But Yomi, bursting into uncontrollable laughter, laughing like she hasn't in months, falls out of line. As the monks scold her repeatedly all Yomi can think about is the last time she laughed like that, loose and carefree, the kind of laugh Eric has always inspired. She says goodbye to the monks the next morning. Her instincts, sharpened by all the meditation and pure diet, guide her south towards Bali with Eric's letter tucked among her things. Following his trail deeper into Southeast Asia, she releases her gaseous drug into the sultry air as she goes.

In Singaraja she tracks Eric down with a kind of desperation he's never seen in her before, risking her life to dive down to Kaliana's lair without the assistance of an oxygen tank, where she brings Eric's sexual sabbatical to an abrupt end. Yomi and Kaliana almost erupt into a vicious cat fight of intense proportions before Eric, donning his scuba gear, pulls his screaming wife out through the red curtain doorway. Back up on land the couple agrees not to discuss the specifics of what they've both experienced during their separation.

But Eric has no way to hide the fact that Kaliana's two primary effects on him are a penis that's almost doubled in size, and a fiercely intense desire to reproduce. The latter will come to threaten both his sanity and his relationship with Yomi. He vows to make it his primary goal, as soon as their mission is finally complete, to fully awaken his wife's passion, to stir her desire for procreation. He sees that his only hope in accomplishing this will be for her to abandon science for a period of time, to treat it like a drug she needs to get off of in order to experience a certain side of life.

During their reunion on the beaches of Thailand, Eric takes note of Yomi's distinct jealousy over his time spent with Kaliana. He, on the other hand, is far from insecure about whatever happened between her and Rupert Jones at the monastery. There is only one thing that his wife can do to bring out his jealousy – leave him for the laboratory. Holding her while the surf licks their toes, waiting for everything to feel right again in the space between them, Eric hopes he can keep Yomi away from her lab with the assortment of skills Kaliana has taught him. After all, he's already an extremely rare and desired commodity in this altered world they're creating – a man with both the ability, and the urge, to procreate. At the same time Eric is perpetually caught off guard by this strange new push from within, a tug that's both strong and gentle, persistent like the pull of an ocean tide. A devotee of spontaneity, his natural reaction is to give in to these sudden urges, so he decides to treat the warm waves coursing through him like a surfer, straight on, with the cocky confidence of a twenty-year-old hot shot.

Dear Yomi

I wanted to write you by hand, because I'm sick of email. The fact that you implied that you've engaged in sexual acts with a chimpanzee in your last cyber-message will nauseate me every time I sit down to write an email. That said, I'm writing you this letter to inform you about my imminent arrival at your doorstep (if you even have a door). Protesting will be of no use – I've already bought the plane ticket. The least you can do is scribble me some directions so I can locate you before the lions and tigers find me! If you don't send a map I'll just sniff you out. My nose remembers you better than any other part of me (except one, of course!)

Your Husband,

Eric

- Letter Eric sent to Yomi in Africa.

New America is trying hard to find itself. The young country is a cultural stew, bubbling in a rolling boil of passionate, free-minded people. Intellects and imaginations blend together as the future of civilization is played out on a small scale, while the rest of the world reels from the impacts of AMLS. Billions of men are regressing into little boys. Women in the Middle East are revealing their faces. European ladies have lost high heels and other impractical clothing choices in exchange for running shoes and office jobs. In Indian villages the women have begun plowing the fields and chopping the wood, leaving the cooking and child care responsibilities to their suddenly meek husbands who wait for them at home. U.S. Environmentalists who haven't yet left for New America are rejoicing at what could prove to be a long-awaited solution to the global population crisis. Christian politicians are declaring AMLS either to be the work of the devil, or of abortion rights and birth control activists gone over the edge. Amidst this chaos thousands of liberal thinkers, professors and artists and NPR listeners, are making their way towards New America in hope of finding an oasis of common sense. Not everyone is let in. Having reopened its citizenship to the world around, overqualified applicants like Bono and Salman Rushdie are migrating there. But the most common immigrants, by far, are frustrated American women leaving behind their AMLS-infected husbands to make a pilgrimage to the new country.

When Yomi and Eric finally return to New America, weary and worn out from their journey, their mission is essentially complete. It's been almost three years since that first dive in Ashokan, when over a million men were dosed in a single afternoon and they'd popped a bottle of Dom Perignon in the Motel 6 that night. A lot has changed since then, for both their foster country and their relationship. Rifts are rising up within each. In New America, a gap has arisen for economic reasons. Half the population feels that it's time to court those U.S. corporations still on the fence about joining the Alliance of Corporate Partners, companies like Wal Mart and General Electric. The rest of the people, on the other hand, wish to remain economically aloof from this tug-of-war over billions of dollars, to focus on growing an economy independent from the rest of the world, one not based on a currency. The first group feels that it will take too long to rebuild their depleted budget internally. The U.S. has encouraged most of the world's superpowers to boycott anything produced by New America, effectively limiting exports to Third World nations. But something has to happen soon - the experience funds are dwindling, and many of the wealthiest new immigrants had their money seized by the U.S. government once their plans for relocation were revealed, for the CIA has made New America it's primary focus, gaining access to up-to-date immigration data. In the midst of these potentially crippling divisions the country comes together to throw a party for their two beloved scientists, icons of the infant nation.

Yomi and Eric plan a renewal of their marriage vows as a kickoff to this welcome home party, an event that takes over a month to plan. During this month Yomi ignores Eric's repeated requests that she let go of both her experiments and birth control. She insists upon remaining on the pill, and returns to her on-site lab with renewed passion. At first she claims it's because she misses her chimps.

"Set them free, then," Eric pleads. "We'll keep them as pets, I don't care – what else do you need to discover in there? You've accomplished exactly what you wanted to with your life, Yomi. You changed the world."

"I know, I know," Yomi says. "But now there are problems – teenage boys are killing themselves – women aren't strong enough to run entire nations, and men aren't caring enough to be proper homemakers. So I need to tweak things in other ways . . ."

"Tweak things?"

"Yes. First of all, the women will need more testosterone in order to have the strength for their new roles. And the men will need more of what every woman has."

"Estrogen?"

"Exactly."

"You're crazy."

Yomi fires him a cold glance.

"Hey, I'm not the one who was locked up in a mental hospital, am I?"

Defeated, Eric hangs his head.

So Yomi returns to her lab in full force. At first Eric accompanies her, thinking maybe he can share this world of hers. But when one of the horny, sexually repressed female chimps grabs him through the bars of the great cage, groping madly for his crotch, Eric runs out screaming while Yomi erupts into laughter behind him. During the days and weeks that follow, in response to her resulting sexual withdrawal, Eric's own sex drive unleashes itself with fury. Like an artist hooked on the high of creative mania, he's consumed by the desire to recapture the bodily euphoria Kaliana had induced in him on a nightly basis. Knowing Yomi waits for him to fall asleep in bed before slipping out for her lab, Eric begins pretending to drift off by changing his breathing rhythms. Once his wife is gone he heads out like a nocturnal predator. He can almost smell the women who are within the five or six day span of their heightened fertility period for the month. He crawls in through open skylights cut into the ground, whispers his way into their warm, soft beds, and pleasures them to degrees most of them had been fearing they'd never experience again. Losing touch with reality, Eric indulges in this animalistic behavior for weeks. The howling screams of orgasmic women pinned to their beds by his oversized member ring out into the nights, wild calls that are answered by the local wolves. All of this is happening just as he and Yomi are set to renew their vows as a cap to their enormous welcome home celebration.

The party is a full week of reveling that starts out pure, with inspired speeches given by members of the Inner Circle, and enormous potluck buffets of the freshest food the nation can produce, before gradually descending into reckless debauchery. By the week's end Arnie is bench pressing a baby grand piano while Elton John strips to a g-string on top, an enormous crowd cheering them both on. Oprah organizes a mud-wrestling tournament, men versus women. Martha Stewart whips up cream pies to be smashed in the faces of the losers, turning their naked bodies into abstract collages of white and black. But even amidst this revelatory chaos most of the guests are able to pick up on the distance between the celebrated couple. Hillary is often seen having long, emotional conversations with Yomi off to the side. Eric forms new friendships with Mark Reynolds and Ben Clarkson, the three of them bonding over beer and talking about the trials and tribulations of being thirty-something men. The party ends abruptly on the eighth day when Eric, in the whirling spiral buzz of homemade sake, announces to the crowd of partygoers that he and his wife are getting a divorce. It's the first time Yomi hears the news, over loudspeakers in front of thousands of her admirers. Eric rambles into the mic, admitting his late night prowling sessions over the past month and revealing the identity, much to their horror, of the five women he's been clandestinely involved with lately, and how he hopes to marry each and every one of the them in the near future.

"The Mormons've got the right idea, damn it," Eric slurs into the microphone. "Polygamy is for me!"

These are his last words before passing out in a heap onstage. Mark and Ben, shaking their heads, haul him away while the party rapidly disintegrates.

From the depths of his ensuing depression, camping out on his man-made island in the middle of his man-made lake, Eric comes to terms with the fact that he's completely lost his relationship with water, and consequently with himself. He no longer dances naked in thunderstorms or daydreams about being a salmon swimming up a waterfall. Worst of all, instead of staying up long hours in the night worrying about how there will be enough water to sustain humanity, he's been obsessed with making babies, spreading his seeds like dandelion fluff in a summer breeze. What's happened to his discipline? He asks himself this question over and over. Devoting his life to Yomi's goal has set him so far off course he can hardly believe it. In the beginning, when he first agreed to help her, he'd convinced himself that the success of their mission could be water's best shot at ultimate survival, because women would make sure it was saved. As Yomi sinks further into her delusions Eric gradually feels his own purpose rising up in full force. Needing to escape the physical and societal burden of his sexual attachments to so many women, he applies to the Experience Committee for a grant to reconnect with water. He receives it without delay.

When Yomi enters Hillary's abode a few days after Eric's drunken announcement to thousands that he's ruined their marriage, she is struck by a twinge of jealousy at the sight of Beth-Ann helping President Clinton execute a half moon twist, a particularly challenging yoga position. Yomi always regretted the fact that she'd turned down Hillary's repeated invitations to join her on the mat. That's why there is sex, Yomi always told herself, because if making love didn't relax her enough it would be time to find a new lover. Except now, with Eric having run off in pursuit of his abstract dream to save water, humiliating her in the eyes of the community by leaving behind three pregnant women, Yomi isn't getting any lovemaking in at all. Even her chimps are noticing her sexual tension these days, and have been keeping their distance from her in the lab.

"Doctor, you look horrible," Hillary exclaims, untwisting her body.

"Thanks. Listen, I need to talk to you – "

"Okay," Hillary says, standing up on the mat. Beth-Ann shuffles her feet.

"I think you'd better . . ." Mrs. Clinton begins.

"Right," Beth-Ann spurts, moving for the door that opens to let her out.

The two women sit down on the yoga mat. Hillary cocks her head to one side, softens her eyes, and waits for the distraught scientist to speak.

"Eric left me. He told me I'm crazy to want to go back out for more . . ."

Hillary nods, taking her time to reply. Her role as a political sage has taught her to be patient in all aspects of communication. Millions of people are often poised on her words.

"Are you referring to your pending requests for funding to dose women with testosterone and men with estrogen?" Hillary asks.

Yomi nods.

"Well, that does sound a little crazy, Dr. Nguyen. And, at the same time, totally reasonable, based on what's already taken place."

Yomi perks up.

"What makes you say that?" she asks the President.

Hillary shifts her position, rocking forward on her pelvis.

"It's like humanity's influence on the natural world, Yomi. We messed it all up, pushed things into one extreme - so now we have to push it in the other direction, which in the end will hopefully restore the perfect balance we disrupted. I think you're doing the same thing with the human race, by tipping the scales so dramatically in the direction of women. I thought this needed to happen, to even things out between the sexes once and for all – that's why I've supported you – but it's time to stop, to leave the rest to nature and let things play out for a little while."

Fearing the intensity of Yomi's reaction, Hillary stands up and makes her way into the kitchen. Yomi sits rigid on the mat.

"I don't agree one bit," she hisses between closed teeth.

Hillary peers into her open refrigerator while she speaks.

"Maybe things weren't even all that out of balance between the sexes. Maybe it was simply that the wrong men had the power, because I've known an awful lot of good men, men I would trust to lead me, men like your husband, and mine."

"Speak for yourself," Yomi scoffs, rising suddenly to her feet. "My ex-husband, you mean, and soon to be father of three illegitimate children – you think a man like that is anything close to the guiding light of a strong woman?"

Hillary is pouring them two glasses of iced green tea. For some reason her usual censor, the screen between her mind and her words, drops away for a moment.

"Maybe you're just a lesbian gone haywire, Yomi. Have you ever considered that?"

"I cannot believe you're calling me a lesbian."

"Why not?"

Hillary stirs honey into the glasses of tea now resting on her marble table.

"I changed the world – but I'm not finished," Yomi snarls.

"Iced tea?" Hillary offers, picking up one glass for herself and nodding down at the other one on the table.

"I have so much more to do – I'm leaving tomorrow – to start the estrogen dosing."

"Not if I veto the acceptance of your requests for funding you're not."

Yomi moves to the table, her muscles taught with anger.

"You can't do that!"

"Yes I can. And I will."

Yomi lifts the iced tea and splashes it into the president's face.

"I'll find the money myself," she stammers, storming out the door in a flurry. Hillary, sticky and soaking wet, picks up the phone and calls her head of security to calmly arrange for Yomi, and her chimps, to be permanently removed from New American territory. After making the call a part of her regrets the impulsive action. Although there have been rumors circulating about the nature of her relationship with Beth-Ann, it's the possibility of something happening between her and Yomi that Hillary's been fantasizing about lately in the more remote corners of her brain.

The president is out back at the ranch, walking through the yard he's let grow up into a field of native prairie grasses. He's even encouraged his neighbors to do the same. But Yomi and Eric, knowing the president to have been successfully dosed following their infiltration of the White House well, avoided much of the Midwest, a region they would have stuck out in like a pair of penguins in the desert. Not to mention the area's high concentration of wells, a fact that would have made any thorough dosing impossible. So most of the men here are still set in the traditional, Republican mindset, which includes the rule that the only grass worth growing besides wheat is the classic lawn grass of backyard America. In gentle defiance the president is letting his thousand-acre parcel revert back to its native vegetative growth. Vibrant hues of yellow, orange and green abound. He has his landscape crew maintain a few interconnected pathways through the sprawling fields of what are now five-foot tall grasses and wildflowers. Sometimes he and the children play hide-and-seek for an entire day, when no one is found until darkness threatens and ushers them all towards the house. Today the kids are napping inside. The president walks the soft pathways, barefoot and alone, thinking.

He's been thinking more these days than ever before in his life. New thoughts stalk him all day long, descending in sunbeams and rising out of bird calls. His mind wanders into realms it hasn't ever acknowledged before, and he loves it. He never wants to go back to his office in D.C. Today the clear blue skies are inspiring thoughts of his wife. She left him almost two years ago and has yet to return. It's not her cooking he misses, or being inside her. What he longs for is the warmth she created in their bed. And he misses his best friend. Something in his brain tells him that if he returns to his old life in the White House she will return simultaneously. But when he lets his children know about the prospect of heading back to D.C. they protest adamantly. They are scared to go back to all the flashing cameras and escorted rides to school. At the ranch, left free to explore, they've discovered things they never knew existed, the smell of grass and clouds in the shapes of animals. Left alone for all this time, unrestrained by concrete walls and standardized exams, the three kids have discovered magic, what they'd previously thought only existed in movies and books, the stuff of made up stories. They've been making up their own stories out in the prairie fields, imagining myths to explain where they came from and where they're going. In this way they impose just enough order on their world to bring it within their grasp and give it meaning.

Both of the president's boys have been dosed by the drug while living in the White House. One of them is ten years old and shows no effects, since his body is producing minimal testosterone at this point. The other boy, Sam, is thirteen going on fourteen. Just before drinking the contaminated water his voice had deepened, hair had begun to sprout from the dark corners of his body. The effects of Yomi's drug are most dramatic in the millions of boys his age. One potent symptom as their bodies halt the process of becoming men is acute depression. Although Sam doesn't kill himself like many others his age are, some days suicide is all he can think about. While his younger brother and sister dance and skip and sing among the field grasses, indulging in freedom, he lies on his back and watches the clouds. For weeks the shapes he sees are horrifying; menacing creatures ready to swallow him up and cart him off to hell. Instead of feeling the classic, healthy urges to rebel, to sink into silences at the dinner table and strike out on youthful adventures of the body and spirit, Sam looks forward to family dinners and reading in his room.

Eventually Sam emerges from his dark cloud hallucinations. He becomes the leader of his two siblings, guiding them through the grasses, bringing along wildflower field guides and scientific texts, writings of the great philosophers, the poetry of Emerson and Longfellow. Not influenced by the overwhelming hormonal bursts that boys his age normally undergo, Sam's young, agile mind is set free to hone in on the deepest of thoughts. He spends long hours pondering the nature of beauty and the destiny of humankind. By the time the family is ready to return to the White House, Sam's confidence has blossomed in full. Unlike many boys his age, he hasn't surrendered to his manhood being taken from him just as it's beginning. Inspired by the prairie and the ghosts of Native Americans, instead he's transforming himself into something close to a genius, one who will grow up to be the kind of man Yomi never envisioned as a potential outcome of her dosings. The teenage boys with the most inner strength, boys like Sam, are weeded out from the weak majority, the ones who can't handle the effects of AMLS at such a sensitive age. These boys will rise above, through the power of their cultivated, disciplined minds, to become the best leaders the world has ever known.

When the president tracks his kids down one fall afternoon out in the fields to tell them that it's time to return to D.C, they want to run away and hide, but know this isn't an option. So they surrender peacefully and climb on board Air Force One the next morning without complaint. Once back in his white palace the president is more restless and unhappy than ever before. Without the soothing effects of the Great Plains out his back door, the scenery he'd come to rely on for peace of mind in the midst of the chemical changes going on inside him, without his children's laughter as the primary soundtrack to his days, he slips into a deep depression. He misses his wife more than ever. Assaulted by his cabinet and the reporters, everyone eager to know about his strategies for combating the mysterious disease that's crippling the nation's industrial economy and altering the entire structure of society, all the president can think about is finding his wife. After devoting many hours pondering her whereabouts he thinks he has a very good idea. So after only a week back at work he asks his children if they want to go on an adventure to British Columbia. They answer in shouts of excitement and bags packed in a flash. The four of them leave the following dawn in a rented Land Cruiser, slipping out of the White House without being followed, heading north towards the territory of New America.

Rupert Jones, world famous independent reporter and New American citizen, restless ever since returning from Nepal, takes a break from his work on the book about Yomi and Eric. He files a request with the Experience Committee for funding an assessment of the United States from an aerial viewpoint. After receiving the grant Rupert makes a return trip to NPR's headquarters in D.C., the network he no longer needs for exposure, where he hopes to gather resources for the survey. After barely convincing the doorman to let him up the elevator, the executives on the top floor order him to leave immediately. They admit that the network has recently gone private and joined the Alliance of Corporate Partners, and if it were to be found out that they were interacting with a citizen of the nation of defectors their membership status would be threatened.

"You're simply having a mid-life crisis," the new CEO tells him. "Go get yourself a real job and stop acting like some born again hippie. We all have to do what we can to survive in this crazy world."

Rupert is stunned by the new attitude of the only network he thought had some kind of a conscience. Taking a detour on his way out, he sneaks up to the rooftop helicopter pads, where he convinces one of his old pilot buddies to take him up for a survey of the state of the union from a bald eagle's point of view.

The pilot is Rupert's friend left over from his happy days working the only news network he's ever respected besides, maybe, the BBC. David Frank has a spirit Rupert respects, turning down the thousand-dollar bribe no matter how many times Rupert offers it.

"C'mon, man, it's an honor to be chauffeuring you around the skies – shit, you're the most famous reporter since, like, Walter Cronkite or something."

Dave straightens the panama hat he wears for every flight as he lifts the chopper up and over the rolling green Appalachians.

"Well, you're the best helicopter pilot I've ever worked with."

"Thanks, man."

"And the most stoned," Rupert adds.

"Hey, you know the smoke steadies my hands. I told you that, right? I mean you've heard me talk about flying Brokaw over the 911 ruins back when I was with NBC!"

Dave twitches in reaction to the memory. Rupert lays a steady hand on his shoulder.

"Easy, boy. Smoke all you want – and forget that day - from what I know of Tom I'm sure it must have been hell. But you'd better watch out now that this network has sold out and gone corporate – they'll probably be testing your piss pretty soon."

Rupert's eyes open to take in the sprawling fields of the Midwest opening up beneath them. He inhales deep and slow.

"Seriously, Dave, is there something I can do for you in return for this?"

"You can get me into New America, that's what you can do. I want to move there, but I hear the border is closed."

"It is. But I can get you in no problem. I know Hillary Clinton. We've done yoga together! She loves me."

"You do yoga?"

"I did. Once. With Hillary Clinton."

"Cool. I've always wanted to check that shit out."

Dave Frank pulls a joint out of an inside pocket of his wool jacket.

"I swear you must have been a hippie in a past life," Rupert remarks.

"Thanks, man."

From the sky, watching through telescoping binoculars, the renegade reporter sees men and children in backyards, in parks, fields, and forests, playing games or building lean-tos or making art. Some of them are simply studying a certain aspect of nature, stalking a butterfly or inspecting the structure of a flower. On the roads there is little traffic. Most of the cars he does see are packed full with groups of women car-pooling to the offices and factories. Trains and buses are filled with women. Using the network's advanced surveillance equipment, even as night falls Rupert is able to watch these working women exchange chocolate and books on their way home. He listens in on their easy conversations with the helicopter's radar devices. Hours into the aerial tour, he begins to notice how the overall pace of the nation has shifted from a high- speed rush to a gentle flow, like the difference between driving the autobahn and paddling a river to get from point A to point B. And it seems that the women setting this new pace aren't at all concerned about making it to Z. The only ones missing, from Rupert's perspective, are the adolescent boys. Most of them are locked up in institutions, debilitated by depression and suicidal urges. The others are gathering in secret basements and forest forts, engaging their minds in long discussions, plotting, without being conscious of it, their eventual takeover of the nation. But for now the women rule. They reign over every aspect of metropolitan life, from entertainment to public works projects to the offices of corporations and governments. In the country side, where wells are abundant, nose-to-the-grindstone farmers and loggers and miners still work long, hard days. The situation makes Rupert think about bees. These country men are worker bees fueled by unhindered springs of testosterone, sustaining new hordes of women, the queen bees now running the show in every city and suburb.

As they near the University of Colorado stadium outside Boulder, Rupert has Dave slow the chopper down. The entire arena is filled with women. Focusing in on the stage through his binoculars, Rupert sees how the rock band is also made up entirely of women. The lead singer is very pregnant. Above the stage a large banner flies reading MOM-BAND FEST I.

"What's a mom band?" Dave asks, still stoned.

"Seems pretty self-explanatory," Rupert says, reaching over to hold the chopper's wheel as he hands Dave the binoculars. "Here, take a look. The lead singer's pregnant, and there's a playpen behind the stage! I think everyone in the band is a mother."

"Wow," Dave says, taking a look for as long as he dares. "What's happening to this country? I don't think there's a single man in the entire stadium! That means there's fifty thousand women listening to a bunch of mothers rock out!"

"Wild, huh? Even though those two scientists I was telling you about definitely sped up the process, I think this was happening anyway, women taking things over and stuff – it's pretty cool, huh?"

"I guess."

Dave hands back the binoculars as he banks up and over an approaching mountain range.

"But where can guys like us find a refuge?"

"New America."

Dave wrinkles his brow.

"Don't worry, I'll get you in."

The next time Rupert Jones returns to the U.S. he will have temporarily let go of journalism to once again travel the back roads, this time selling newly invented robotic vacuum cleaners door-to-door, making his next round of contacts while strengthening old ones, accepting invitations into living rooms where another breaking story might await his discovery.

The first place Eric Underwood heads in his journey to regain his connection to water is the aquatic biology department at Cornell University, where his infatuation with the element first took hold of him while earning a PHD in watershed management a decade before. He lives out of a hotel in downtown Ithaca for a week, spending his waking hours talking to students in the hallways and tracking down his former professors, most of whom are still working out of the same cramped and stuffy offices. The level of excitement that had defined the department during Eric's years there has vanished entirely. The students are unenthusiastic – the majority are trying to transfer to schools in other countries. The professors with tenure are just hanging on for the sake of their families, while the younger teachers are trying as hard as the students to leave. Dr. Randall Wilson, Eric's mentor, explains what's going on while the two of them visit the machine Eric built as part of his graduate thesis, a device that captures the rain and converts it into double the volume of drinking water by encouraging the splitting and recombining of hydrogen and oxygen molecules. Dr. Wilson polishes his glasses with his shaggy tie. He mentions that the machine has just been shut down for the first time since Eric's departure from the program.

"What's happening to this school, Randy?" Eric asks the man he still respects more than anyone he's ever met.

"The same thing that's happening to every science program across the country – the government is cutting all funding down to the last penny, and most of the private sources of money have been absorbed by your country. We can't even pay the electric bill to keep your wonderful machine running."

Dr. Wilson shakes his head of bushy white hair. Eric kicks at the ground in frustration.

"So what do you think is in store for water here in the U.S.?"

"That's a much worse nightmare than the education horrors – it seems the government is in the process of privatizing all sources of fresh water, including the rain – water will be their optimum tool in controlling the masses. Soon it will cost as much, by volume, as a fine Bordeaux."

Dr. Wilson lays an arm across Eric's shoulders.

"My suggestion is that you head back to your country and worry about yourself, your family, and your friends. It just doesn't pay to try to save the world from its problems anymore, Eric."

"It never really did, did it?"

"Almost. Us hippies almost got a ball rolling that might have been big enough to save it all, but we came up a little short, so we had to put on ties and get paying jobs."

"Too much free love and reefer," Eric jokes, attempting to lighten the mood. The professor chuckles under his breath. Eric's mood refuses to lift.

"Wanna grab a beer?" he asks his old teacher, although he knows even a beer and a view of all the university girls in town isn't going to raise his spirits either. He just wants to kill time until the next day, when his week at the hotel will be up and he can take himself to the Adirondacks. There he'll camp out for days, where the desire to reconnect with his watery worlds, with the mystery of dragonflies and the innocence of minnows, will get him out of his sleeping bag every morning, where a pack of Skoal and a campfire will put him to bed each night. There, bonding one last time with the place he gave up for Yomi and her project, he'll bid a final farewell to his lakes and his streams, to his Adirondacks.

Once Eric has satisfied his back-to-nature experience in the Adirondacks, after crying into the lake waters during tearful monologues expounded before his audience of loons and shooting stars, he returns to what has become, by default, home. He starts living in a teepee he's erected on the island in his lake, one of the only above ground dwellings in all of New America. As he settles back in his friendships with Ben and Mark grow. Their relationships solidify around certain things. Mark fills the two others in on what life is like as a man with AMLS, giving long-winded, detailed reports on his condition. He tells them about not wanting, or caring, about sex, and how utterly relaxing that is, although he admits it might have been the primary factor in the downfall of his marriage.

"Oh yeah, for sure," Eric agrees. "If there was some way to measure it, you could easily prove that women are way hornier than men – they need that dark, empty space filled up on a regular basis – wait, are you saying that you can't get it up?"

Mark nods, heavy with embarrassment.

"Not even while we were watching Salma Hayek rehearse that nude scene on Set B last month? 'Cause that was hot - "

"Not even then," Mark admits, hanging his head.

"I'd rather be dead," Eric announces.

"What else has changed?" Ben asks Mark.

As Mark expounds upon his peculiar state of being Eric suffers through twinges of guilt over what he's done to his friend, and so many millions of other men that are now just like him. Mark speaks of his increasing attachment to his children, how they, and other children he encounters, are the only people he wants to spend any time with. Children make him comfortable with himself in a way nothing else can. He describes his inability to plan ahead beyond the next few minutes, how he cooks when he's hungry and sleeps when he's tired, which is often. But what ends up contributing most to Eric's guilt is the fact that Mark now wets his bed on a regular basis, another humiliating side effect to which most AMLS victims eventually succumb.

While the former lawyer tags along and shares the disheartening symptoms of his condition, Eric introduces Ben to the world of water, leading his two friends on treks to the sources of creeks and the melting tips of glaciers. Ben, in turn, takes Eric and Mark deep into the old growth forests, where he explains the subtle language of trees and how to manage them for both profit and sustainability. In a dark conifer forest one afternoon, while Mark chases chipmunks and scampers over boulders, Ben talks about the *mamas* in Colombia and their relationship to water.

"They listen to the force of *Aluna,* the idea of life that originated from the warm waters of creation to become the pure force of human thought. They're watching the ice retreat up the sides of their mountains and the springs dry up. They're predicting the same thing you are, that the world will run out of water – and, just like you, they believe that saving it will save everything else."

"I'm losing touch with that belief," Eric mutters.

"No you aren't," Ben says. What he hasn't told anyone, even his wife, is that after his mountaintop experience with the *mamas* he started acquiring their ability to read thoughts. So he knows Eric isn't thinking the words he's saying. Eric wants to hear specifically how these nature priests are attempting to reverse water's dire fate, but he won't ask out of plain stubbornness. He secretly likes being the renowned scientist gone awry with disillusionment, guzzling home brewed wheat beer and reproducing at the pace of certain rabbit species.

"They're trying to save it with prayer," Ben states, answering the question his stubborn friend is refusing to voice.

"Oh."

Sara Reynolds, left alone in their suburban mansion in Greenwich, at first relishes her nine to five schedule. She enjoys the peace and quiet at home during her hours after work, without the dirt and ashes from the backyard invading her living room, without sticks and leaves accenting her shag carpets. But now that she's working forty-plus hours a week there is little time to worry about the cleanliness of carpets, no motivation to maintain a home for her husband and their children. Sara lets the house descend into a chaotic state of mess and disarray, ordering take-out most nights because whenever she tries to cook she misses Mark with such unexpected intensity her tears keep salting the pans. She worries about him driving across the country with their boys, and torments herself with guilt over how she treated him after he contracted AMLS, something that hadn't even been his fault. She misses his goofy innocence, his childlike enthusiasm, the breakfasts in bed.

After a few weeks of happy employment at City Hall, Sara is starting to think something very wrong lurks beneath the perfectly pleasant atmosphere the women have established inside the town's governing offices. At the end of the work day, after all the easy conversations and shared baked goods, meetings outside and breaks to call husbands waiting at home, Sara realizes they really haven't accomplished much of anything since the men quit. But when she mentions this obvious lack of productivity to Laura Johnson while they share a scone in the office tearoom, her friend shrugs it off.

"What is there to get done, Sara? We all make a sacrifice just to show up for the day, to take a paycheck home every week so our children can eat. Isn't that enough?"

Sara stares at the floor.

"But, before, when the men were here, things were happening in town, projects were being started, like the pedestrian-only street."

"Everything's different now, Sara."

"Well, it's not going to work without men, Laura. There's no contrast, no opposing forces, the tension between the sexes that has brought us to where we are now – it's all gone, and we're stagnating. That's my take on it anyway."

Sara breathes hard after her passionate outburst. Laura swallows the last bite of scone and washes it down with her tea, scanning the offices, looking for a sign of what her friend is talking about.

"Maybe you're right," Laura finally says, her voice hardly burdened by concern.

Sara is worried to a point almost beyond her control. Without saying goodbye she walks straight out the back door. As she heads for her car in the parking lot, she decides that it's time to find a different job, one where men and women are working together, where things are getting done. She'd heard in Rupert's piece on NPR how some men have been spared by the roving team of scientists. These men have learned to channel testosterone into fuel for purposeful activities, like music and art and growing food, rather than the destructive outlets of war and greed, or the blind pursuit of a corporate career. They have to be out there somewhere, Sara thinks. There has to be a place where these last real men are working alongside women, a place where the key aspects of civilization, things like culture and politics and forward growth, things Sara has always lived for, must still be alive. For all she is concerned her town, left solely in the hands of women, will die a slow, if serene, death. But after heading out on the road that very afternoon, Sara quickly discovers that most of the real men left in America have packed up and moved away. The ones that stay, like Mick Johnson, keep their unexplainable immunities to themselves as they stick to the routines that sustain them.

Laura Johnson's husband Mick still makes it to work. He's avoided Yomi's drug because he never drinks water, or coffee, even. He only drinks whiskey and beer, in which the high heat of fermentation disables Yomi's drug. Mick Johnson doesn't drink to excess, really, but alcohol's effect on him always increases his bitterness towards life. The couple usually meets at his favorite bar a couple evenings a week. The dive is miles outside the suburban center of town, all worn wood, with the tobacco stains from years past streaking the walls. When they walk in this afternoon Mick struts up to the bar with his characteristic swagger, the cocky gait that would make any stranger certain he's much more than a car mechanic. His torn blue jeans, long white hair and cocky strut are the getup of a real rock'n'roll singer. Mick Johnson always wanted to be the lead guitarist of a famous band. But he still rehearses in a garage and plays low-paying gigs in out-of-the-way bars on random Saturday nights. The bartender, a chick he's never seen working before, the only woman Mick has ever seen tending the rough-hewn bar since he began frequenting it a decade earlier, slides over to take his order. Laura heads for the bathroom, where she'll stare into the mirror and splash water on her face in an attempt to prepare for the next hour and a half, biding her time until they get home and she has Mick all to herself. Then, with no one to impress, she knows his roughness will finally dissolve, revealing the man she originally fell in love with.

"What'll it be, sir?" the bartender asks.

"Please don't call me sir – I'm anything but a 'sir'."

"Okay."

"Jack on the rocks for me, sweetheart, and a red wine for the lady, the cheapest stuff you got, 'cause she'd never know the difference anyway."

"Don't call me sweetheart," the bartender says as she moves to pour the drinks. "I'm anything but sweet."

When Laura emerges from the bathroom Mick's torso hangs over his drink. It's the posture of a man who likes liquor a little too much. He lifts up as she slides onto the stool to his right and cups her hands around the wine glass.

"Cheers, baby," he says, raising his glass into the air.

"Cheers," she answers as they clink glasses. He sucks down half his drink while she takes a gentle sip of the cheap cabernet, trying not to wince at the sharpness of the tannins. Her palate for wine is actually quite developed, something her husband has never made an attempt to acknowledge. They chat about their days for a while like a normal couple. Laura tells him about Sara's crisis moment in the tea room earlier that day. Mick tells her about being the only guy at the shop now, how overworked he is but how much money he's making them at the same time.

"Thank Jesus I haven't caught this disease all the men seem to be – "

"Shhh," Laura says, placing her finger over his lips. "Don't jinx yourself, hun."

"Yeah, good idea."

Mick catches a flash of color to his left. He turns to see a twenty-something local kid who recently burst into the music scene, with an upcoming tour across the Northeast. Mick was Joe Fleece's guitarist a few years back. The kid still had a lot to learn back then, and looked up to Mick as a mentor of sorts.

"Hey Fleece, I see you've graduated to bourbon straight like a real rock'n'roller, instead of drinkin' it on the rocks like a wuss!"

Joe Fleece turns slowly to face to couple. He makes eye contact with Laura first, who smiles and sends him a friendly wave. Then he focuses on Mick, lifting his eyebrows when he speaks.

"A little bird showed up at one of my shows a while back and chirped some advice into my ear – told me what to eat and drink in order to avoid contracting this AMLS thing."

Joe leans towards them to whisper the last part. "Fermented drinks are fine, but tap water, and drinks on the rocks therefore, need to be avoided at all costs – I even keep my mouth shut in the shower now – I brush my teeth with bottled water."

Mick scoffs.

"Listen kid, I'm not about to change, not at this age. I don't touch water anyway – got no need to drink something that ain't gonna kill me slowly – brush my teeth with oil and grease - but I always sing in the shower, and that'll never stop."

"Suit yourself," Joe says, swiveling back to face the bar.

"And guess what?" Mick prods. "I could sing any one of your

songs a hell of a lot better than you can. In a shower or on a stage, it don't matter."

Following that stinger Mick rises, lays a kiss on Laura's taut neck, and saunters off towards the bathroom. Joe, always sensitive, still lets himself be affected by Mick's abrasive nature. Laura can see it in his face.

"I hope you know he doesn't really mean that – booze goes right to his head. He'd do anything for you if it came down to it."

"Yeah, I guess," Joe admits.

That night Mick takes his usual before bed shower, scrubbing off the day's grime and belting out Joe Fleece's country rock tunes at the top of his lungs, proving to no one but himself that the kid has more talent than he ever will. Mick tilts his head back to sing straight up into the streaming water. He lets it splash around in his mouth and down his throat, scoffing at Joe's advice at the bar. That night he sleeps fourteen straight hours without moving. He's diagnosed with AMLS the next day.

Yomi, broke and hiding out in a dingy apartment in backwoods Maine, has been unable to go forward with the second and third phases of her mission. The chimps are everything, the only thing she has. She spends day and night with them, wallowing in the sadness of a dream turned nightmare. The chimps are depressed too. They miss their cage in New America, one that had surpassed Yomi's original setup for them by far, with a bamboo forest, two creeks with pools for bathing, and special lights designed to imitate the tropical sun of equatorial Africa. But the last round of experiments altered them in strange ways. In the dark and shabby apartment out in the middle of nowhere the chimps are heavy with sadness, pissing and shitting on the cracked linoleum floors, ripping the stuffing out of couch cushions and raiding the refrigerator whenever Yomi falls asleep. Yomi rarely goes out, choosing instead to stagnate on her torn couches covered in orange hairs, watching television and eating Doritos, refusing to believe that she's suffering from the effects of a broken heart.

One gray, midwinter day, desperate to rise out of her despondent situation, she sits down at her laptop and starts writing out a grant application. After numerous online searches she comes up with a list of organizations to send it to. A few weeks later she hears back from EARL, the Exotic Animal Rescue League, a nonprofit based organization in San Francisco devoted to returning exotic animals to their original homelands. EARL agrees to fund the transport of her chimps back to The Congo. Yomi convinces them to allow her to accompany the animals on their journey home. She makes no plans to return, hoping to become the Diane Fossey of chimpanzees. Bringing the chimps back to their jungle home in this altered state is a total experiment. She knows the wild chimps will, at the least, refuse to accept these effeminate males back into their macho-based society. She can only hope that the bonobos on the other side of the river, recognizing a similar laissez-faire approach to life in these testosterone free males, will grant them entrance into their social ranks. Even if it takes Yomi choosing a temporary mate among the wild bonobos to facilitate the process of gaining their ultimate trust, she'll do it. Yomi comes to terms with this fact on the flight. She figures what the hell, chimp love can't be much different than sex with Eric. He's almost as hairy as a chimpanzee, and likely grunts just as loud during the act.

With Yomi's recent departure from New America, Beth-Ann seizes the opportunity to get closer to Hillary. They begin doing yoga together regularly, drinking iced green tea afterwards and talking intimately about their problems with the men in their lives. Beth-Ann's husband, now the former President of the United States, gives her daily fodder for dissatisfaction as he continues to suffer from the effects of AMLS. He hardly resembles a man anymore.

"I don't know what to do with him, I mean, he still wants to keep our marriage going, as if nothing has changed – I have to admit, he's an excellent father to the children now, it's just . . ."

"That a woman has needs?" Hillary interjects. Beth-Ann nods with reluctance.

"Maybe my husband should take care of your needs."

Beth-Ann grimaces as Hillary continues.

"This testosterone drug might do Bill some good – apparently he has way too much of that hormone – as the whole world knows his sexual overdrive almost ruined my entire career, and he's not showing any signs of slowing down. I can't keep up with him anymore. Besides, I'm not even sure it's a man that I want these days."

Beth-Ann snaps to attention. Lately, around Hillary, she's experienced certain fantasies she would never admit to anyone.

"What do you mean?" she asks. Her innate innocence causes Hillary to burst into laughter.

"I mean, I think I might want to be with a woman now – I tried it out in college, while Bill was trying pot – it was okay, but maybe I just wasn't ready for a woman's love . . ."

Beth-Ann tries to stop her gaze from wandering into the folds of Hillary's blouse, her eyes from following the shaded counters of the president's still-perky breasts. If she could hitchhike and enjoy it, Beth-Ann thinks, trying to look away, could she also enjoy doing something other than yoga on Hillary's mat? The only problem is, the person she's idolized over much of her adult life seems to have another woman on her mind.

Driven by the guilt from his role in disrupting the human balance, Eric returns to science in search of some kind of retribution. He reopens Yomi's lab with the goal of working on discovering a cure to her drug, what no other scientist the world around has been able to come up with. At first being in her space invokes a pain of reminiscence too strong for Eric to be very productive. He knows his way around the lab from the time he spent in there during his effort to become familiar with the world that had always been her true home, a phase that had ended abruptly following his molestation by one of the sex-starved female chimps. Once Eric overcomes the burden of memory he settles into the space with ease. With a clear mind he's able to think back to something Yomi shared with him during the early days of their dosing. Nearing the end of her research she stumbled upon a version of her drug that negated the very effects she was aiming for, a slight variation that would revive the dormant hypothalamus of a dosed man into producing testosterone once again. As usual she shared these details with Eric, and his scientist's mind hasn't forgotten the formula. It takes him barely two weeks to recreate this substance in the lab using samples of the drug Yomi left behind when she fled New America so abruptly.

His first patient is Mark Reynolds. The treatment goes smoothly, and Mark quickly returns to a close version of his former self. But before taking on any of the thousands of New American citizens with the disease, men who are literally banging on his door, Eric decides to start a flower garden. He plants in the ground above the house he shared with Yomi. While sowing the seeds, watching the flowers emerge and grow at their own steady pace, a slow build-up to the blooming that might only last a day or two, he learns new things about love. His mind quieted by soil and water, Eric begins to acquire a new definition of the deepest human emotion, a definition much different than the one Kaliana had taught him.

His new understanding of love is centered on the concept of growing inspired by his flower garden. Thinking back on his relationship with Yomi, he can see the love they grew over time, the slow development visible only to the ones doing the watering and weeding every day. At night, struggling to hang on to peace of mind, he torments himself with guilt over the fact that he ripped up the roots of their love just as they were finally starting to take hold. This fact threatens his peace of mind on a daily basis. With the rest of his spare time, seeking distraction through physical labor, he builds huts elevated on stilts above his lake in a style based on the indigenous building techniques he observed while traveling through Fiji with Yomi at the tail end of their mission. He builds six of them to be exact, one for each of his five wives and the last for him, a place to spend one or two nights a week recuperating from the efforts of maintaining marriages with so many women.

Following his successful rehab, to the dismay of his boys and the elation of his wife, Mark returns to his former self with renewed vigor. After Sara accepts his invitation to come to New America, he designs and helps construct a sprawling underground home for his family. The first piece of furniture he buys is a leather chair, which he sits in to drink his Johnny Blue, neat. He interacts with his children primarily at the dinner table, just like he used to back when he worked seventy or eighty hour weeks for the Manhattan law firm bearing his name. He and Sara start having sex every morning. He accepts an offer from President Hillary to become the nation's chief legal advisor, as lawsuits from the U.S. government continue to pour in on an almost weekly basis. His first case, ironically, is to defend Eric Underwood against charges brought on by the United States regarding the scientist's role in assisting Yomi with her contamination of the country's drinking water sources. He wins the case easily, and quickly becomes the most sought after lawyer in New America.

Even after witnessing his wife's transition into lesbianism and the successful rehabilitation of Mark Reynolds, the former U.S. president ignores Beth-Ann's persistent urging that he seek out Eric's testosterone therapy. Out of work, with plenty of time for reflection, he's been overwhelmed with guilty thoughts over some of the political decisions he made during the course of his leadership of the most powerful country in the world. From his new position of clarity he can see that his move to go to war in the Middle East was inspired by fear – he'd been scared of going against the desires of the oil barons who had funded his campaign. And, with the image of a tough cowboy to maintain, he had feared appearing weak in the eyes of his country. So he resurrected his father's old enemy and started a war in the desert, one that still lives on in the daily bloodshed of suicide bombings and insurgent attacks. Having been raised Catholic, the ex-president is quite familiar with the concept of guilt. The inherent shame of this guilt is what's driving him to purposefully remain a victim of AMLS. Like a good Catholic, he feels the need to be punished for his many wrongdoings. So he packs up his wife's frame backpack and wanders off alone towards the Selkirk Mountains, hoping to suffer in the glacier snows, hoping a wolf might gnaw off a limb.

Feeling his extended state of sexual overdrive wind itself down, Eric remembers a quote he once heard from someone, or read somewhere, that declared loving another person to be the most challenging thing a person could ever do, how everything else in life is simply preparation for this ultimate goal. Eric can't help thinking he's failed his shot at this for the final time. And it feels like he won't get another opportunity. Through the 20/20 lenses of hindsight he can see how, during the years before Yomi came into his life, he was in love with a landscape. Wooing the Adirondacks, he was content to slow dance with pine-covered ridges and remote ponds, writing love poems to the stars. But like his mother always tells him when one of his mad obsessions starts driving him towards an unhealthy edge – *divorce it.* He divorced his underwater worlds of upstate New York for Yomi. But what has he left her for? No matter how madly he's ever reported loving her, his mother would never advise him to divorce Yomi. Blind from his running away from her he's left a trail of burdens in the form of five wives, all of whom he's still trying, rather unsuccessfully, to fall in love with. And, worst of all, Eric stops enjoying sex altogether. His only comfort and sense of companionship comes from being under water in his man-made lake, although even then it isn't long before his mind wanders helplessly into the dead-end memories of Kaliana and the sex-infused air of her coral cave.

Craving clarity on what to do next, Eric takes a trip up into the Selkirks to commune with the source of the Goldstream River. After two days of hiking he sets up camp in a high alpine grove of aspens just below the snowfields. There he waits for some kind of clear direction to emerge from the leaves quivering in daytime breezes, from the sharp stars splattered behind the canopy at night. Waiting, letting certainty build up in waves, he dreams about Africa whenever he sleeps. On his fourth and last day in the aspen grove he's snapped out of his heightened state by the sight of a man in ragged, torn clothes stumbling through the trees, bumping into the skinny smooth trunks and spinning in haphazard circles. Reluctantly, Eric rises to approach the man, now collapsed in a heap on the soft forest floor. Holding his torso in his lap, Eric can tell it's the former President of the United States, a man he's never respected and has purposefully avoided since moving back to New America.

"What are you doing here?" Eric asks the barely conscious former leader.

"I came here to die," is his weary answer.

"Well, it looks like you're doing a good job of it – I'd say you're very close to succeeding, in fact."

"Good."

"Talk to me, man – why do you want to die? I mean, it sounds cliche, I know, but there really is so much to live for, don't you think?"

"No, I don't. Not for me. I screwed up too many times – I'm responsible for so many lives lost, innocent lives – for the continued destruction of the planet – I could go on and on confessing my sins, but what's the point, really? There's no such thing as salvation for a man like me."

"That's not true at all. My mother always tells me that it's never too late to change – where is your wife, she must be worried sick abo – "

"Eh, I doubt it – we don't see much of one another anymore. I don't satisfy her, I guess. I think she likes women now, anyway. Whatever."

Eric lifts his eyebrows.

"That's right, I have AMLS. Thanks to you and your crazy wife."

"Ex-wife. And she's not crazy. She's a scientist. Listen, I'm sorry about that, but I've just developed a cure – I really think you should give yourself a chance at being cured – then you can make a clear decision about suicide, from a real man's perspective. Trust me, without testosterone your mental chemistry is totally fucked up – there's no way you're thinking straight these days."

The former president nods, then passes out in Eric's lap.

Shortly after his trip into the mountains Eric wakes up alone one morning in his bamboo-stilt hut above the choppy waters of his lake. He's been spending his nights solo, hiding from his wives and battling a severe depression. Trying to block out the sound of strange helicopters buzzing by overhead, after brewing a cup of cowboy coffee on his backpacker's stove he checks his e-mail. The only message of note is from Yomi. The subject line reads *Greetings from The Congo.* Although the tone of her e-mail is lively and upbeat, Eric knows his ex-wife is feigning happiness, perpetuating an unspoken competition between them as to which one can find the most joy in the aftermath of their relationship. As if such a thing can be measured, Eric thinks, shaking his head as he reads her words describing the inner workings of chimpanzee society. In her last line she admits to finally being pregnant, alluding that her child might be of a genetic makeup never seen before. *You fucked a Chimpanzee?* Eric writes in the first line of his reply, then deletes it. He's struggling to let his truest emotion rise up. He feels sorry for Yomi, sorry that she will always be trying to find the sense of contentment she knew with him but didn't acknowledge until it was too late. The thing is Eric has done the same and he knows it. He can't relax. Lying in the arms of all his wives never adds up to the satisfaction he knew on a daily basis with Yomi, how their interlocking bodies felt like home no matter where they happened to be. Instead of telling her about the communities of algae in his lake, or updating her on his experiments in her old lab, Eric launches three simple words through cyberspace.

I miss you.

When Yomi writes back a few hours later she invites him to Africa for a visit. Her bait, what causes Eric to buy a plane ticket that evening, is the chance that the baby might actually be his. She ends the e-mail with three words of her own, poking fun at herself, something Eric has never known her to do before.

I l-uff-ove you.

The three friends are seated at a round corner table in The Brown Liquor Bar, a pub recently opened by Mark Reynolds, a relaxed joint serving only bourbons and whiskeys and scotches. The bar is situated on the south facing shore of Eric's lake. Sipping Knob Creek on the rocks, they gaze into the setting sun angling through the bamboo bungalows perched on stilts, the Selkirk Mountains rising jagged and snow-capped in the distance. As soon as Eric mentions his plans to head for The Congo to track down Yomi a hush descends over the table.

"Why do you want to do that?" Mark asks. "The woman's crazy, and you have five of the most quality wives any man could want."

"She's not crazy," Eric blurts out, defending Yomi's sanity once again.

Ben studies his friend's face, listening to his thoughts while Mark asks another question.

"She's pregnant, isn't she?"

Eric nods long and slow. Mark shakes his head back and forth, turning to ignore Eric by speaking only with Ben. Eric gets up and leaves the table. No one will ever truly understand him, he thinks, except one, the woman who dissected his heart as if it were one of her experiments.

Like Gary Nelson, Yomi's first and only boyfriend, Eric has been thinking he can look forward to a life spent living with one memory lurking in his subconscious, a director's cane ready to snare his waking mind at any moment with the jolt of an image from the past and yank him off the stage. The image is a specific look on Yomi's face, a look of acute distrust. Eric sees her crumpling face in the middle of a sea of people at their welcome home party, right after his drunken announcement of an infidelity on the most horrific of scales. He's haunted by this image – his spirit is yanked back continually to the memory of it just as he nears the next potential pinnacle of his life. Ever since their split Eric sees himself futilely knocking on the door of happiness but never to be let in again because he lost track of Kaliana's Golden Rule – he stopped showing up for love. He made nightly escape attempts, slipping out of their warm bed to slink into the chilled night, prowling for heat from other sources. Yomi always left the bed first, of course, but only to pursue her elusive science, an inherently innocent part of her makeup. Loving Yomi, Eric had known from day one, meant being able to love the scientist side of her, something he'd accomplished by letting her have it all to herself, by not trying to understand it. With eighteen hours of traveling to get there, Eric will have plenty of time to ponder the reason he's heading to The Congo to track down his ex-wife in the jungle. He thinks that by the time he arrives he'll have a pretty good idea why. And, he thinks, he might never come back. Consumed by a curiosity for the aquatic biology of the Dark Continent, taking one last shot at love, he has a one-way ticket.

Just before Eric's departure for Africa the U.S. based Alliance of Corporate Partners, in their push to secure the polar ice cap as a privatized source of fresh water for U.S. citizens, invades the territory of New America. Their hope is to destabilize the young nation's strong allegiance to Canada before continuing on to the North Pole. Mr. Walken's virgin army, one he purposefully trained to engage solely in honorable, hand-to-hand combat, has no way to defend the attack being made in digitized aerial strikes. The citizens huddle in their underground dwellings while the ground rumbles and shakes all around them. Resisting the urge to surrender, Mrs. Clinton visits the former U.S. president in the hospital, where he's recovering from his near death experience in the aspen grove. Hillary crouches by his bedside in the middle of the night. Streaks of color flash through the sky, visible beyond the ground-level skylights above, flares that remind her of fireworks. Placing her hand on the ex-president's shoulder she shakes him awake. He mumbles into the darkness.

"Where am I?"

"The hospital," Hillary answers.

He sees her for the first time, her face illuminated in sporadic flashes of yellow, orange, red.

"Oh yeah, that's right, I almost forgot. What can I do for you, Mrs. Clinton?"

"First of all, I heard about what you went up into the mountains to do, and I want to say that I'm sorry it got to that point – for my part, I just wanted to recommend yoga as a great way to combat depression."

"Listen Hillary, I'm a cowboy from the Midwest – riding my horse and shooting my guns is what I do for therapy."

Eric's treatment, administered only days earlier, is already having a drastic effect on his personality, piecing back together the original fragments of his manhood.

"Fair enough," Hillary says, leaning back as the former leader sits up. "Well, the reason I'm here is because, in case you're not aware of it, while you've been in the hospital our country's been invaded by the United States of America. The head of our military is urging me to surrender."

"Military, heh, you don't have a real military, Mrs. Clinton. No offense or anything, but you know as well as I do that Christopher's ninjas don't stand a realistic chance against any First World nation's attack. Listen, this country has grown on me since I arrived, and even though I was hardly a man then, I really have no desire to return to the man I was – or to the country I once led. So, if you're asking me to help, the answer is yes. I'll call up some of my friends, friends I made on my own terms, not my father's – friends like the great nation of Israel, with the most respected military in the world."

"Thank you," Hillary whispers, trying to hide her surprise.

Israel's air force responds by swooping in the next day to push out the corporate-backed military without a single round or missile being exchanged, succeeding on intimidation factors alone. Following an apology by the Alliance of Corporate Partners, signed by The Colonel himself, relative order soon returns to New America.

The Colonel swivels in his leather chair, kicks his feet up on his shiny silver desk, and gazes out his great windows at the Houston skyline. Recently appointed chairman of the board for the Alliance of Corporate Partners, the Exxon CEO is trying to overcome the surprise of their recent defeat in British Columbia. The plan that he and his oil boss buddies came up with a couple years ago, to drive the price of gasoline up by inciting a series of hurricanes along the southeast coast, is having the exact result they'd hoped for. The poor, unable to drive or even afford the rising cost of public transportation due to the fuel shortage, are finding themselves unable to make it to work. The ACP hopes to create a permanent economic gap between the haves and the have-nots. One thing they couldn't have foreseen, however, is the domination of American society by women, a fact that is threatening their entire scenario of corporate domination of the lower class. Leaning forward, Sanders clicks his desktop to reveal a revenue chart for Exxon. Since the dramatic spike at the time of the floods on the Texas Coast last year, the seventy-percent jump in earnings that will go down in history, profits have been declining steadily even as gas prices have risen. He can feel the blood pounding in his temples, his frustration swelling as he thinks back to all the news reports of late, images of women carpooling to work; four, five, six women piled in hybrids, women filling the trains to capacity. Something has to be done about this, Sanders decides, swiveling to face the skyline once again. The Alliance, having just failed in their attempt to invade New America, must make it a priority to reverse this trend before it's too late. It's time to find a cure to this castration disease at whatever the cost. After making a few calls to some of the Alliance's sharpest, most informed advisors, it becomes clear who they need to find. They find him in the O'Hare Airport, forcing down a cup of Starbucks while reading the latest issue of *Thirst*, waiting for his flight to The Congo.

Before Eric knows what's hit him he's been whisked away from the less-than-comfortable chair in the terminal to an extremely uncomfortable prison cell. He doesn't know it, but he's in a former government lab built into a mountain outside Los Alamos, New Mexico, what the Alliance has recently converted into torture chambers to replace a now defunct Guantanamo Bay. He squirms awake in the cold concrete darkness. Metal pipes clang, reverberating through the long, dark hallways. After some hours have passed Eric still has no idea if it's night or day. His cell has no windows. At some point he hears the footsteps of cowboy boots approaching down the hallway. A quick shiver of apprehension passes through him. He's never met a cowboy, but for some reason distrust is the first emotion inspired by the sound of The Colonel's boots on concrete. George Sanders unlocks the cell door, steps in, and clangs it shut behind him.

"Who are you?"

"They call me The Colonel."

"Pff," Eric says, almost spitting in the oil baron's fat face. "Like Colonel Sanders the chicken man or something?"

Sanders shuffles his feet, boiling with rage over his nickname being insulted.

"Let's move on," he says, sitting down on the stained, flimsy mattress.

"Good idea – why the hell am I here?"

"Because . . .you have something we want."

"And who is 'we'?"

"The Alliance of Corporate Partners – have you heard of us?"

"Vaguely . . ."

"Well – why don't you sit down, you're making me nervous for Christ's sake."

"No thanks."

Eric continues pacing back and forth in front of The Colonel.

"Fine. Anyway, due to our high level of connections, our board members were alerted to your little tap water project just in time – most of us have been able to avoid ingesting this horrible drug – I have to admit you two were quite . . .pervasive with your technique – not to mention rather sly. But getting back to the point, what's happening to American society, and to societies around the world, is just not acceptable to us."

"What do you mean by acceptable?"

"I don't know if you noticed, but thanks to the two of you, women are now dictating the course of the major economies, something that's absolutely detrimental to the Alliance's plan. The reason you're here is that we heard you've developed a cure."

Eric had seen this coming, and recognizes the need to think fast. Having finally shed all his spur of the moment tendencies and the short-term perspective of youth, he's come to terms with the need to be selfishly practical above anything else. Sharing his cell with The Colonel, Eric realizes he's never been this close to a person controlling so much money. And he likely never will be again. So he sits down on the ragged mattress.

"Make me an offer, then," he says, stroking his beard, feigning a businessman's toughness.

The next day Eric is back on a plane heading for The Congo, a multimillionaire ready to believe in monogamy. He only hopes Yomi will forgive him for selling out to the Alliance. He has a feeling she won't care.

Eager to make his own contribution to New America, Ben decides to fully detach himself from his cherished yet isolating worlds of literature. To accomplish this he arranges with Mark Reynolds to stock a corner of the Brown Liquor Bar with all his books, sporadically underlined, with cracking spines and pages folded in both corners. The act doesn't terminate his relationship to books, only changes it. He begins recommending titles to people in the community, selecting works he thinks the individual will connect with and relate to. The celebrities come to him as if he's a shrink, as if the books he selects for them are new pills to try out in order to combat depression or anxiety. He doesn't sell them, but loans them out like an unofficial librarian. Ben finds a surprisingly deep satisfaction in this role. When his books are returned and he connects eyes with the reader, both of them acknowledge the same journey taken. They share a few of their favorite scenes, comment on lines of dialogue or use of metaphor. In this way Ben, simply by removing them from his living space, distances himself from books and increases his connection to them at the same time.

Without her role as a priest to pour herself into, while her kids are immersed in the multi-layered New American educational system, Maria wanders through the days searching for something to grab onto, wondering if she'll ever hear God's voice again. What she does hear during her hours spent roaming the plains, or sitting by the banks of the Goldstream River, is her own inner voice telling her that the skies have been unusually clear for weeks, the river is lower than she's ever seen it since arriving a year before, and the supposedly permanent snows on the Rockies in the distance are retreating, leaving behind bare rock and sliding mud. What she can't know, what Rupert Jones long ago informed the Inner Circle about, is the Alliance's method of producing rainstorms by using sonar aircraft to induce massive evaporation over The Gulf of Mexico.

This atmospheric manipulation is resulting not only in the severe hurricanes that have been bombarding the coastlines of Florida, Louisiana and Texas, but also a dramatic shift in weather patterns across the entire North American continent. Although Maria is the first citizen to notice it, soon all of New America watches with horror as the grasses wither to a dull brown in the midst of spring becoming summer. Soon there isn't enough water for the people to drink and to feed the hydroponic gardens and free-range game at the same time. The air is dry. Lips crack on pace with the soil. Eric's flowers go limp under the relentless sun. Without a currency-based economy, importing water or produce and meats from other nations is not a viable option.

The Inner Circle calls an emergency meeting. The women leaders spend days brainstorming a solution, throwing out ideas like building an aqueduct to channel the retreating snow line of the Rockies, or digging deep wells in search of hidden aquifers. At one point Oprah speaks up. She remembers the presentation made to the Experience Committee by a couple from Vermont the year before, a report on a group of Indians in Colombia. She remembers the culture was centered around water and prayer.

"There's a couple living here - they were in Colombia last year visiting some Indians dwelling in the mountains by the coast. According to them, these natives can talk without speaking, and believe they maintain the balance of the planet with their prayers and their intimate relationship to water. Maybe they can make a storm cloud too, and send it this way. What the hell, it's worth a try, right?"

Oprah feels the curious stares of the women. She has no idea why she's just said this. Maybe the subject of Indians caused her mind to wander naively into the concept of rain dances. Either way, once the meeting is adjourned it's decided that Hillary will speak with the couple about the possibilities of getting some kind of help from the *mamas*.

A few days later, seated on Mrs. Clinton's yoga mat underground, Maria talks with animation about their experience in Colombia.

"They have faith," Maria says.

"Faith," Hillary repeats, uttering the word like it's the name of a past lover.

"Do you have it?" Maria asks.

"I do," Hillary says. "Although it often doesn't feel like it – I just know I have faith in something . . .something bigger than myself. Otherwise I never would have made it here, where I am now, because I've been so alone during most of the journey. Alone but never lonely, really."

Maria nods slowly. She speaks in her calm preacher's voice.

"A person with true faith is never lonely."

"Do you think they can help us?"

"I do – if we help them."

"How can we do that?" Hillary asks.

Maria tells her exactly what needs to be done.

The next day the Experience Committee, at Hillary's direct request, releases the most money ever given to a single project for the Tayrona church construction. The grant will also be used for purchasing all remaining tracts of the Indians' homeland, and to fund the protection of the boundaries of this sacred land from the paramilitaries and cocaine farmers. Ben, free from the confines of literature at last, leaves promptly for Santa Marta with a check for five hundred million dollars. Maria is happy to stay home to watch over their children and his dog. In return for the donation, Ben will ask the *mamas* to build an enormous rain cloud with their accumulating prayers, one that will be able to reach the desiccated plains of New America in enough time to revive them.

Two deck tables are occupied at the Brown Liquor Bar. Hillary and Bill Clinton sit on one side of the expansive porch. They're on a date. Holding each other's hands, they speak in soft sentences. On the opposite side Snoop Dogg rolls a spliff and sips a gin and o.j. while Bill Gates, seated across from him, drinks mineral water with lime.

"So, you and Melinda been to Africa, ain't that straight?" Snoop asks.

"Straight?"

Gates wrinkles his brow as he struggles to understand the rapper's lingo.

"Shit, you know what I mean, geek-boy – I'm sayin' is it true you guys have been to the homeland, the Dark Continent, the Nile Jungle Pussy of human origination?"

"Yes, we've been to Africa, Melinda and I – numerous times, in fact. The place is an enigma, a dichotomy of beauty and misery."

Snoop sparks his spliff, leans back and puffs down for a minute straight, shrouding both of them in a cloud of thick gray smoke. When it finally clears Gates has an obvious contact high. He fusses with coasters and cocktail napkins while Snoop takes in the mountain view.

"Damn straight."

"What?"

"Nevermind, whitey. But seriously, what is it you're saying, this enigmatic dichotomy shit?"

"All I'm saying is that I love Africa. And I want to save it. Okay?"

Snoop sits up. His hands fly when he talks.

"Save it from what? Capitalistic empires like the fucking United States?"

"From itself, Snoop, that's all. From itself."

Snoop Dogg relaxes a little.

"All right."

"We straight?"

"Hell ya', we straight."

"Good."

Gates waves his hand at Mark Reynolds as he emerges from inside and heads toward the Clintons' table.

"I'm hungry," Gates says, patting his stomach.

"'Cause you baked, homey. You contacted a high."

"Yeah, well, either way, I'm ordering up some food . . . "

"Hey, could you get me a little somethin'?" Snoop asks politely. "My fat rolls of cash are worth nothin' up here . . .Time to start hustlin' all over again."

"The hustle never ends, Snoop."

Mark Reynolds, who pours the drinks and manages the bar while his wife Sara cooks old home New England-style dishes in the kitchen, brings the presidential couple two cognacs. After stopping for a bit to chat with them about the drought, he moves on to his other two customers on the opposite side of the porch. Hillary and Bill peruse the menu, browsing past selections like Hot Turkey Sandwiches and Mac & Cheese. After the date, as they've both agreed to call it, they will go back to his place for sex, when Bill will howl with pleasure after not getting any since their last date the month before; when Hillary will go numb, her mind wandering to a continent she's never visited, to the woman she accidentally fell in love with. Bill has been wondering if his wife's distraction of late is the pressure of her presidency finally starting to take its toll, or if it's something else. They used to have these kinds of dates once a week.

"Being a president isn't all it's cracked up to be, is it, hun?" he asks her as their cognac glasses meet in the air.

"It's not that – I love my job. I wouldn't trade it for anything."

There are no limits to the term of a New American president, and Hillary has no plans to retire any time soon. She is the most influential woman in the world, and her duty to maintain this position drives her onward through the days.

"It's just . . .I miss someone, that's all."

"The crazy scientist, you mean?"

"She's not crazy . . .just very – passionate."

Hillary has trouble keeping anything from her husband, and hopes his finely tuned perception hasn't honed in on her attraction to the Japanese chemist, something no one else would ever have been able to guess.

"You want her, don't you?"

Hillary sucks in a quick breath.

"What makes you say that?"

She feels like she's sitting across from a Supreme Court judge. She won't be able to lie to him.

"I just know, Hil – I know you better than anyone."

He has her there and she knows it. This is why they have the dates every month. Even from her lofty position of power Hillary has to always check back in to the sides of her that only her husband knows, sides that will stay dormant without him in her life. While the cognac tickles their toes they drop the menus to hold hands across the table. When Mark comes to take their order she asks if they can have the food to go.

"You ask me that every month, Mrs. President," Mark says, glancing down at Bill, lifting his eyebrows.

"I know – it's some kind of ritual or something."

"I understand. So what can I have Sara whip up for you guys?"

On their way out of the Brown Liquor Bar with their to go boxes the presidential couple lingers in Ben's corner of used books. After a short time browsing they both come up with a selection. Bill chooses *Siddhartha* in an effort to continue his literary exploration of the mystical worlds his wife reports accessing through her yoga practices. Hillary pulls down a hardback copy of *My Life*, her husband's biography that she's never actually sat down to read, hoping his insight on himself might help her fall back in love with him. Mark checks the books out himself from behind the bar since his unofficial librarian is in Colombia building a church.

Alone in his office, the lights of the Houston skyline reflecting through the great windows, The Colonel studies a projection of his company's gas profits on one wall, a downward sloping line of slipping cash flows superimposed on the polished mahogany. The national newspaper on his desk has a bold front-page headline – **THE END OF OIL?** The Colonel has known the death of black gold was coming. That's why he's been urging the Alliance to focus on water. Failing to acquire the polar ice cap has been a major setback. The storm cloud technology is a noteworthy achievement, but, for some reason, he feels it threatened. The pestiferous Jones reporter is probably already sniffing it out, Sanders thinks. He takes a swig off a bottle of Smirnoff stashed under his desk, wipes his lips with the back of his hand, then rummages through his desk for a cigar even though there is absolutely nothing to celebrate. He comes up empty, finding only the stumps of past stogies smoked in celebration of the record profit margins of recent years, before AMLS ruined everything. Buzzing his secretary, screaming into the intercom, Sanders remembers that she left to take an executive position with a hydrogen fuel cell company. Most of his employees, and all of the women, have now left to accept better positions with alternative energy companies following his refusal to allow Exxon to branch out into these arenas. He clicks the power point screen to the next projection, which shows sales of the Alliance's patented cure for AMLS. The profits are a flat line at the bottom of a chart. Men, it appears, are choosing to remain infected with the disease. Or, more accurately, their women are making this choice for them. After recently taking majority control of both the Senate and Congress, they initiated amendments in an attempt to control the actions of any men not infected with Yomi's drug by limiting their rights. Although many of the farmers and artists still left in the country understand the need for this, The Colonel, and many other corporate big shots just like him, cannot accept the new laws.

When he reaches under his desk a second time his hand seeks something other than the bottle of vodka. The cool steel of the pistol feels good to his fingers. But he wants to die another way. His skewed mind decides that what's given him his life should be what takes it away. Leaving the gun and the bottle behind in his office he makes his way down to the parking garage and heads out in his Lincoln Town Car. He drives the lonely highway to one of his father's largest oil fields outside the city. After nodding at the guards by the gate he drives his luxury sedan over the rocks and sand, parking beside a lit-up steel drill plunging rhythmically into a gaping hole in the ground. Stepping out of the leather interior The Colonel strides across the cement foundation of the rig and stares down into the churning crude. He takes in a deep breath of the raw smells, the molasses and tar fumes that always transport him to his childhood. Pinching his nose shut as if he were jumping into his swimming pool at home, he hops off the edge. The oil swallows his body, fills his lungs and stomach, churns him into its heavy blackness. His screams are muffled into silence.

The Colonel's only son, a twenty-three year old boy who has lived his life in his father's substantial shadow, finally makes a leap into manhood following the oil king's elaborate funeral. He forces himself into a version of forty days and forty nights in the desert, camping out in the corporate headquarters for a month with nothing but the basics, bread and cheese and water. Brad Sanders is inspired by his need to see what course of action to take now that so much responsibility has landed in his lap. When this month is up, after taking control of his father's fortune, Brad declares his goal to make Exxon the leader in the corporate acquisition of freshwater resources. But in order to accomplish this he'll have to work alongside the women now controlling practically every aspect of society. Occupying the empty building himself, he paces the floors like his father's ghost, scheming into all hours of the night. His first move is to import the team of engineers that designed and constructed the rainmaking technology in New Orleans to come and occupy the company headquarters for a few weeks. He turns one floor of offices into a temporary hotel for these visitors. He instructs them to begin work on smaller-scale versions of the systems they've been using in the Gulf of Mexico. His plan is to set these up on a rotating basis at the municipal reservoirs he's currently purchasing with his father's substantial financial empire.

In a month's time the engineers have completed designs for portable evaporation machines, elliptical discs like the ones attached to the hovering planes that can be transported by large trucks and set up in a day's time on the banks of America's largest lakes. These land-based systems will produce smaller versions of the gulf coast storms. If Brad can build enough of them, and buy enough reservoirs and other large bodies of standing water, he thinks he'll be able to control the rainfall patterns of the entire United States. Then, once this project is up and off its feet, with competent people installed to run it, he'll shift his attention to drinking water. Even with the Alliance's acquisition of Eric Underwood's cure to AMLS, the majority of the U.S. population refuses to drink tap water now that it's been revealed to be the vehicle for contracting the disease. Just like his father had predicted around the dinner table and at board meetings years before, a fierce competition for freshwater has arisen between both corporations and countries. Brad is already working closely with U.S. military people to develop glacier-harvesting ships to compete with the fleets already assembled by other nations, as well as by the Ice Pirates that have begun harvesting chunks of the melting polar caps for sale on the lucrative black market. Brad hopes to have a fleet of ships ready to stake claim to thousands of tons of glacial pack within three months' time. If successful, although he wouldn't admit this to anyone, he'll have a shot at the kind of power a man like Alexander the Great once knew. Brad Sanders visualizes himself conquering entire continents by controlling billions of people's access to the primary element responsible for sustaining them.

Having grown up into adulthood without ever holding any kind of job besides a few chores around the house that his various stepmothers forced on him from time to time, buckling down into fourteen hour days redefining one of the world's largest corporations is a shock to his system. Brad rises to the challenge every day, and every day he becomes more aware of his father's favorite saying, words of wisdom The Colonel would share repeatedly with any child or grandchild willing to listen.

"Life is like the ladder to a chicken coop – short, steep, and full of shit!"

Another of his father's legacies, one that reached a much wider audience, is Exxon's Promise to the country – *To ensure that Americans will NEVER run out of gas.* One of the first things Brad does is change this into a version reflecting the company's new direction – *To ensure that Americans will never run out of FRESH WATER.* A different resource is emphasized in Brad's version, but the same corporate takeover mentality underlies the new company pledge. Brad Sanders spends long, late night hours hovering over a watershed map of New America spread out in digitized form across the polished black monitor that stretches across the middle of the room like a giant table. The map, constantly updating itself based on rainfall amounts and municipal usage rates, is a high tech, large scale version of the ones Yomi and Eric had crumpled up in a briefcase during their odyssey around the United States of America. Brad stares at the patches of blue lakes and the capillary lines of underground aquifers, wringing his hands together while his mind whirls with visions of H2O domination. He'll conquer sources of water the way a great general would conquer land. At times Brad likes to think it's just a matter of color. Should he go for blue or green? But inside he knows it's so much more than that. Post-AMLS America will not run out of land for many generations, if ever. He's had his people do studies. Water, however, is another story. More precious than gold and diamonds and oil and coal combined, many lives will be lost in the upcoming fight for this most vital resource. Brad Sanders wants to be on the front line of this new war, even if the line is in his office of leather, mahogany, and mirrors. It's the kind of place most of the generals will be this time. Except the only available armies are primarily women and teenagers, and the last thing any of them want to do is help men like Brad achieve his goal.

Weary from days of travel through The Congo outback, bribing military police and following the crude map Yomi sent him, sketched with a coal ember from one of her fires, Eric finally makes it to her community of chimps deep in the jungle. His arrival, and subsequent occupation of her tree house, causes a social upheaval in the tightly knit bonobo society. Some local females are riled up by the attention Yomi is receiving from the males, who have been vying for her affection. One of them even succeeds in becoming quite intimate with her for a period of days. These females eye Eric with distinct suspicion, while Yomi's own chimps stress about the fractured laboratory community and their lack of appeal to the wild bonobo males. Yomi spends weeks trying to set everything back in order, finally communicating to the males, in their language of utterances and hand gestures, that she's entirely devoted to Eric. She even attempts to enlighten them on the concept of monogamous love, and thinks the notoriously promiscuous chimps have begun to grasp this complex emotion from a new perspective. After hiding out in her tree house for close to a month she finally convinces Eric that it's safe for him to descend to the jungle floor.

"Are you sure?" he asks, leaning over the edge, peering down at all the reddish orange heads congregated below.

"Oh yeah – I think I convinced them we're in love."

Eric lifts his eyebrows, not at the notion that the chimps understand the concept of love, but because Yomi didn't stutter over the word she hasn't been able to pronounce in two decades.

"You said love without the uff," he points out.

"I know. Being pregnant has changed me in a lot of ways – I guess that's one of them. Not to mention I didn't speak a single word for a few months here, just grunts and the other utterances of chimpanzee communication."

"What else has changed?" Eric asks, hoping for a specific answer.

I don't long for my lab anymore - I just want to be home."

"Where's that?"

"Here," she says, pulling him close for a tight hug.

"Well, you still have to show me which chimp knocked you up, so I can beat the shit out of him."

Yomi pushes him away, smiling.

"None of them 'knocked me up' as you so rudely put it. The baby is yours. I just thought a little jealousy might get you out here faster."

"It did. I've never been jealous of another man – but somehow a chimpanzee might have something I could never acquire, some kind of primitive manhood I couldn't compete with no matter how hard I tried, you know?"

Yomi snuggles into his solid frame.

"You compete – and you win," she says, carefully stroking his ego in just the right way.

Made in the USA